HE BROUGHT HIS SIGHTS TO BEAR ON THE DARK OUTLINE. . . .

He could make out the legs clearly now beneath the browse line. *A man . . .* His throat became dry, tongue sticking to the roof of his mouth. *One of his own kind. . . .* He touched at the curve of the trigger, forcing himself to recall the shots minutes before buzzing past his head, the dead hunter in the forest, the burning figure staggering out into the snow, the shot ripping through his arm as he dreamt of Joannie. . . . He hunched forward, squinting down his sight, body tensed, finger squeezing, squeezing . . .

"A superb story of tension and suspense . . . characters that Faulkner or O'Connor would have been happy to call their own."

—*The Chattanooga Times*

THE
HUNTING
SHACK

Gunnard Landers

A DELL BOOK

Published by
Dell Publishing Co., Inc.
1 Dag Hammarskjold Plaza
New York, New York 10017

Copyright © 1979 by Gunnard Landers

Dell ® TM 681510, Dell Publishing Co., Inc.

ISBN: 0-440-13300-9

Reprinted by arrangement with
Arbor House Publishing Company

Printed in Canada
First Dell printing—November 1980

To Kathy for being there; and to my mother, Louise Landers, for freeing me from role typing

THE
HUNTING
SHACK

CHAPTER I

The figure in red stood bracketed in the crosshairs of the rifle scope. If only they could know, the man thought, his forefinger shivering ever so slightly against the cold metal curve of the trigger. The smallest movement, a tiny squeeze with his right hand, and the world would explode. Just a little pull, a fraction of an inch, three pounds of pressure . . . He shook his head back and forth, a quick nervous gesture of the joy bubbling at his throat, his lips drawn back in a mirthless laugh. And to think the distant figure didn't even know.

The opposing hunter was turned away from him, on a stand facing down a shallow ravine. Ninety, a hundred yards, he figured, a good distance, all but curtained by a stand of tall frozen hardwoods waving awkwardly in the strong northeast wind. The wind of covering snow, he thought, shivering despite the pulsing of blood through his breast. He shuffled in place, boots crunching softly in the foot-deep snow, in order better to rest his left wrist and forearm against the thick poplar and firm up the aim of the rifle. He squinted across the bleak scene of waving gray trees and motionless snow toward the hunter in red. He moved his head slightly to bring the figure to lifesize in the crosshairs of the scope. The hunter was standing there, looking down the ravine as if that was the only direction from which a deer could possibly come. Some hunter, just standing there all bundled up and shaking in his boots and not the least bit alert. He spat to one side, hard.

Again his finger edged down to caress the curve of the cold metal trigger, a curve custom-designed for his pink forefinger, a perfect fit, an extension of himself—the trigger, the rifle, the bullet. . . .

There'd been a time, the first time, when he'd stood in the forest like this. He recalled it clearly. He'd been in the woods for hours, walking slowly along, pushing his hunting boots through the ankle-deep snow, pausing often to lean against a tree, the expanse of naked trees and snow stretching around him as far as the eye could see. Sometimes he would lean against the same tree for an hour, not overlooking a deer runway, not overlooking anything, just standing in the stillness of the forest, hour after hour, until his head began to hurt and he would drift on, shuffling slowly through the snow, his muscles strangely without strength. His path had meandered. Several times he would walk headlong into low-hanging tree limbs and look around in puzzlement as he rubbed his head and readjusted his hat. Eventually he'd move on.

But then, that one particular day, a snowstorm in the offing, he had spotted a hunter at a distance who, like the one before him now, had been oblivious to his presence. He raised his rifle and gazed through the scope, a game he'd been playing for years, a bit of harmless pretend. Crazy, they'd think. But they had no idea.

Even now, two years later, he hadn't decided whether that first action had been conscious or not. He'd been standing there looking through the scope. . . . The rest of it was blurred, they hovered in his memory, the fusion of the trigger with his finger, the red hunting jacket in the crosshairs of his scope, the ever-increasing caress of the cold metal building, firming into ecstasy, into climax.

The surprise, the rifle jumping in his hand, the picture of the hunter reeling away, the blast echoing with tremendous force back and forth off the frozen trees and jarring his ears until they hurt. . . . Quickly he had brought the rifle back to bear, swinging the field of the scope back and forth, his frenzy growing when all he could see were walls of trees and brush. But then there had been something red, crumpled and unmoving in a foot of pure white snow. At first he had felt no frenzy, only a strange joy, a life within himself that he knew they could never understand. . . .

He blinked—the figure in his scope had turned and was looking directly into his eyes. Mentally, without moving, he pulled back, his scalp prickling as if he'd been discovered in the midst of a crime. But the hunter, a mere boy from the smooth, red-cheeked look, turned back to face the ravine. "Didn't even see me," he whispered to himself.

He touched the trigger again, the crosshairs centered on the distant red back, the lifebeat of his racing heart a joyous pain from the near-discovery. His finger eased back to take up the trigger's slack, pulling against the filed sear lip holding the cocked bolt and poised firing pin in place. He grinned, his teeth barely visible. Just a tiny movement of his finger, just a little squeeze. His mouth opened wider, as though laughing, but he made no sound.

Again he drew behind the poplar, savoring the nervous thrill that ran through him. He was simply looking and thinking, for now. Two years ago he'd done the one, the accident, and then last year another, a body that no one had ever discovered. So a couple of hunters had been killed by stray bullets, one of them never even located. It happened a dozen times every season. He glanced up past the waving, naked limbs of poplars to the gray sky. Time was passing. The others would be waiting. This year he would leave it alone, he thought, a sadness settling deep into his guts.

He glanced one last time through the scope, starting at the picture. The hunter wasn't a boy. It was a girl. He could see clearly. She'd taken off her hunting cap and brunette hair had fallen almost to the collar of her red jacket. She turned to show her profile, the snobbish upturn to her nose, the creamy complexion, the large brown eyes, a libber type, he thought, also thinking that he'd never done a girl before. Out in the woods trying to be like a man. What was the world coming to?

He blinked, focusing his eyes on the crosshairs, their intersection firmly centered, without a flicker of movement, on the red. "Steady as a rock," he thought.

Unconsciously he was taking up the trigger slack, edging against the tiny metal lip that held back the firing pin. How much pressure was three pounds? She turned her head, the skin white, the cheeks red, the one eye he could see clear and bright. She was young, a determined one, he thought. And oblivious.

The rifle jumped, jarring his view. The explosion ripped at his eardrums, ricocheting back and forth off the frozen trees and screaming its message for a mile around.

Panic clogged his throat. He glanced about, leaning forward against the poplar for support, for concealment. But he could see nothing, there was no one. He slumped forward, aware of the painful throb of his heart, of having mainlined himself. A thousand times he'd seen it on television, someone shot dead. But to feel the real thing . . . the real thing. His head jerked with the first spurt of his coming, with the sweat of his slipping the womb. The power. If only they knew.

He shuffled a little circular jig in the snow, a dance to his newfound life. But abruptly he sobered, peering through the narrow opening in the trees to the crumpled red. A girl. "Damn," he said aloud. He hadn't meant to do one this year.

But he had no choice, he realized. They'd asked for it.

Suddenly his eyes widened, confronting the aberration of a ghost. The distant red was moving. He snapped the scope back up to his eye, drawing behind the tree as he did so. The girl was struggling to raise her head and shoulders. He was breathing heavily, the vapor of his breath billowing up and fogging the eyepiece of his scope. Oh God, he thought, and wiped at the lens with his mitten. Sure enough, she was still alive.

He pulled behind the tree, struggling to check the rise of panic, to beat back the fear he'd mastered so well. Gradually the racing vapor of his breath subsided. "Okay! Okay. She's alive," he told himself quietly. "But she can't survive."

Carefully he poked the rifle, and then his head, out from behind the tree. The girl was moving, crawling obliquely in his direction. He watched in fascination through the scope as though watching a movie—her painful drag through the snow, the twisted agony on her face, the bright red blood bubbling down her chin, and the track of blood a foot wide behind her in the snow. She was sure to die, and still she spent herself in a useless crawl, just like a wounded buck who thrashes away from the hunter no matter how badly it is mangled. It was mindless. "Crazy," he said aloud, the sound of his voice startling him this time.

If it was a deer he'd finish it off, he thought, and he brought the crosshairs to bear on the bobbing

head. But as quickly as he touched the trigger he
opened his hand, cursing his brief stupidity. Another
shot would completely ruin the stray bullet theory.
Besides, she'd die soon enough.

He could see that her crawl had all but stopped.
She'd covered perhaps twenty yards and had left a
wide blood trail the entire distance. She pulled her
head and chest partway up on a small fallen log, eyes
squinting, bloody lips curled back, face as white as
the snow around. He stared without moving, without
breathing, watching the young woman's last minutes
of confused agony, the annoying wait dragging at his
newfound life.

The log, no more than six inches high, had stymied
her. She could go no farther. She laid her head in the
crook of her arm and stared out at the snow in front
of her face, blood coming out of her mouth each time
she breathed. After a time her eyes seemed to become
fixed and the blood stopped and her body sagged into
that crumpled state in which he knew life could not
exist.

He breathed gently and glanced around the forest.
He was alone. The first flakes of the predicted snow
were swirling down. Darkness would come early. He
glanced one last time at the fallen girl, every detail
flickering through his mind. Somehow he'd become
larger, possessed of something more than he'd had
when he entered the forest—an awareness of mind
and body he'd never thought possible.

He smiled, a kind, gentle smile of contentment. He
turned and drifted quietly back through the hardwood forest, the snow crunching softly under his
boots. The others would be waiting.

CHAPTER II

Norm Petrie stood on a ridge overlooking a finger of the seven-mile swamp, standing in amidst the shiny green of some balsams. Overhead the brilliant winter sky showed through racing puffs of snow clouds, and for a few minutes Norm basked in sunshine. He was an imposing figure, tall, large boned, his face craggy with deepening lines, naturally tanned, his eyes dark brown, his hair black. He glanced around at the carpet of white, at the naked brush and poplar trees, aware of the dormant life they concealed. He breathed deeply, the pure, cold air an elixir to his lungs.

It was the early afternoon of the opening day of the season, the burdens of his morning with the others behind, the forest his alone. He moved downhill and followed the base of the high pine ridge, slipping almost silently through the brush and snow, his steps short and carefully placed, his weight rolling gently from heel to toe, eyes ever mobile, alert for a hint of life. He carried his rifle casually in one hand, an item necessary to his being here, like the tie and suit he wore out to dinners and cocktail parties with Joannie.

Joannie, such a marvelous creation. He winced,

aware that he hadn't touched her for over two months.

Something, a bream nibbling at a bobber, tugged at the bare nape of his neck, the awareness there before the image ticked in the corner of his eye. Without turning his head or changing his pace, he glanced sideways across the open finger of swamp to a stretch of highland a hundred yards beyond. There, concealed in another clump of balsams, a figure in orange was pointing—he squinted—pointing a rifle . . . at him?

Norm walked steadily, head straight ahead. An angry buzzing reverberated through his mind. What to do? How would it look if he ran? Was the man simply glassing the swamp? Or was he actually aiming at him, like someone had at that girl who had been shot the year before? For a moment he thought of Korea, that bald-headed hill where he had won his distinguished service medal, the nation's second highest award, for refusing to quit his slow, ponderous climb toward those Chinese machine guns. The memory lived, the rape of gunfire, his buddies crumpling at his feet, bleeding, their lives ebbing into the dirt, with no chance of redemption, ever. Seconds before they had lived—and so quickly they had died. If only they had kept moving. . . .

He managed to drift casually toward some cover as if he had noticed nothing, then broke into a lumbering run, digging through the snow until he was out of the watching hunter's sight. As he reached cover he paused and leaned against a poplar, out of breath, rubbing at the solid Appalachian features of his forty-five-year-old face.

"Damn," he muttered, angry at the way his self-control had snapped. Perhaps the blurry figure in red was simply another hunter looking through his scope to see if he was a familiar figure. Or perhaps the man had really been glassing the swamp in search of deer.

And yet, just as surely as a young rabbit smelling a fox for the first time instinctively knows a mortal enemy is near, he knew the forest had changed.

Norm shook himself free of snow. He'd been frightened. He could smell it, a young wolf outbluffed by a wise old raccoon. Such a fool, and in his own forest. He stepped slowly back into the open and, seeing nothing where the other hunter had been, circled cautiously around to where the man had stood. He could see from the spacing of the man's tracks that he too had run. He could not find a clear bootprint because the dry, granular snow had fallen back into the impressions, covering the size and bottom markings.

He stood there for several long minutes. That the man had run. . . . For the most part only guys from the shack hunted this area, although occasionally a stranger did wander through. Why would he run?

Slowly, watching carefully, he set out following the tracks, seeing a spot where the man had fallen in the snow, picked himself up and continued, first at a fast pace, eventually slowing and stopping several times to turn around in a small circle. Norm shook his head, retreating against the headache of possibilities. A stranger? One of the guys? Why the movement like this?

It was early afternoon, and opening day, he reminded himself. There were probably more greenhorns in the woods today than in the whole rest of the season. There would be a logical explanation for all this. There always was. Still, he followed the tracks deeper into the forest.

"Ah, hell," he muttered, the uncertainty of his encounter with the distant hunter feeling like the frustration of his home which he wanted to escape: Joannie in their immaculate house, in her flowing clothes, at their evening meals, the four of them, he leading the prayer, their nights out on the town, he in his modish but ill-wearing suit, out to a dinner, a cocktail party, or downtown for a play, a process of moving from one place to another, then sitting and watching and talking and sitting and drinking and talking. And in between there was work, day after day under those shimmering neon lights, production schedules, parts delays, sick employees, shoddy work, and at the end of the line they had what? A television set before which they spent their lives.

But people said he had it made—beautiful house, beautiful wife, a good job. Big, homely Norman Petrie. They shook their heads at his luck.

And the house was nice, better than he'd once thought he'd be able to afford. Joannie had insisted on the place, taken a job in a department store, worked some nights to help pay for the large split-level with the split-rock fireplace and the split-rock siding and long, sloping yard filled with shrubs and flowers and hedges, all set and trimmed and maintained by his hand. "We don't have to hire someone to do everything for us," Norm told Joannie as he planted the costly shrubbery. "We can do some things ourselves."

"Suit yourself, Norm," Joannie said, knowing that once he set his mind he couldn't be swayed; like the remodeling of their family room in the basement, it was something Norm had to take on himself. "I just thought we could have the nursery do it and save you the work."

The yard work became one of his pastimes, cutting the grass Saturday mornings, trimming the hedges, a chance to get away from the constant cocktail parties Joannie got them invited to where he wore the clothes she picked out and listened politely while everyone chattered their soap operas of other people's lives. And at work, once they made him foreman, the never-ending employee bitching and slacking, the constant pressure from management. They had to do better. And every morning and night, just to start and end the day right, there was the twenty-two miles of hectic freeway driving, bumper to bumper at either sixty miles an hour or ten miles an hour. His head rang with the throbbing of sound, horns, the roar of engines, the choking exhaust, and then into the factory, with the whine of mile after mile of conveyor belts passing through the blue haze of neon lights and gray cement floors with yellow lines marking the aisles. "Mix in, Norm, talk a little." Joannie's terse whisper was in his ear as he stood deep in white shag carpeting, a bourbon on the rocks in his huge hand, the delicate beat of Dave Brubeck filling the background. Yes, he needed that yard, those shrubs and flowers so easily understood, although he did seem an unlikely figure in the yard, tall, dark, with rough features that made people glance quickly away so as not to get caught staring.

But the yard work took only a few hours each week, and then only in the spring and summer. The bulk of his time went to the factory. Day after day, for twenty-five years, he'd been working there making television sets, seldom saying a word, showing up and doing the job he was told to do, never once protesting a change in his duties. "Get Norm," they said if they needed a fill-in. He didn't really mind, if they just left him alone.

Then one day they came and told him he was being promoted to foreman. "Foreman?" He'd never considered it. "Look around, Norm," they said when he quietly questioned their wisdom. "You're the senior man around here. You've worked in every department. You've always done the job. We need you."

He hadn't know what to say. He'd only been trying to do his job, stay out of the way, not make trouble. Why didn't they just let him be? But no, they handed him this, being in charge of other people, employees complaining on one side, management pushing on the other. What could he say? He said nothing and they gave him the job and he went off on his own, figuring things out as he went, never asking for help, supervising as best he could.

And then, just a month before deer season, less than three years since his promotion to foreman, they surprised him with an offer he'd never anticipated: promotion to management level, production management, a high school graduate side by side with all those well-dressed, smooth-talking college graduates. And, abruptly, out of a strange buzzing in his head, without even discussing the matter with Joannie, he'd made the decision. "No. Absolutely not," he said. "No, I won't do it."

He recalled his encounter with Joannie that evening when he told her. She was beautiful, flawless, the joy of his life, along with Kim and Jeffrey, of course. He had stood in the living room telling her what he had done. As he had talked in his slow, ponderous way, the realization of what he'd decided began to take hold.

All that he loved and could never leave. She stared as he talked, eyes wide, a campus queen with short brown hair that shone, and a creamy-smooth complexion. To her, to anyone, he seemed without emotion, standing there calmly, a tall, homely man with deepening lines in his naturally tanned face. He shifted uneasily, isolated in a plush living room with a strange and beautiful woman. She was refined elegance. He was ugly and ignorant.

She shook her head, her thin smile one of pity that he could make such an unseemly decision, kiss off thousands of dollars and a real management position just like that. And without consulting her. "My god, Norm. You poor fool," she'd said in a smooth voice, and walked away, her buttocks tight against the top of the flowing gray slacks, her waist thin underneath the maroon sweater, the body beautiful—but he could not touch.

The memory lingered, the problem still unresolved as, despite everything, he left for his annual trek north to the shack for deer season. He had to, to escape, if only for this one week.

He stared at the tracks in front of him. And now this. What was this? One more thing after his morning with the others: Glenn and Rod taking off on their own, Butch with the illegal doe, up to his elbows in blood and the gray swirls of guts as he ripped inside the backbone at the still warm tenderloins; Merald and his kid, David, with the spike-horn buck David had shot through the ball joints of both front shoulders; Bernie with his bulbous nose, constantly draining his flask and ceaselessly shuffling about as deer ran by unseen at his flank. And even his own buck, a nice little six- or eight-pointer lined up clear in his sights. But again, as he had for the past three years in a row, he'd let it pass. Joannie and the kids wouldn't eat the venison. He had no use for the meat, for the hunt.

The emptiness of it all struck him again and he leaned heavily against a tree, staring at the brown tips of his boots and the snow and frozen ground.

Why would a man be pointing a rifle at him? He roused himself. He could see clearly where the man had passed at the base of a small knoll and then made a fishhook back to the top of the knoll to a stand of brush where he could observe his backtrail. The quivering excitement of this discovery stilled his breath as he searched the desolate winter forest. That a man had seemingly been aiming a rifle at him, and then had run, and now made this little maneuver, like a buck does to watch his backtrail or to lie in ambush. A sharp buzzing pounded at his skull, a vacuum he dared not enter. "Impossible," he muttered, and set out with his nervous energy.

"Just see who it is," he muttered. "Find out what's going on."

But he moved even more cautiously now, pausing often to peer into thickets of hazel brush, toward clumps of pines and the tops of small hills. Instinct told him to circle out, away from the tracks—move off to the side where he wouldn't be expected. But he resisted, staying with what he knew to be proper civilized behavior, a simple misunderstanding that could be logically explained.

The tracks continued steadily into the forest, indicating a steady pace, too fast for sneak hunting. The trail led down a steep incline and into an open finger of the seven-mile swamp, drawing him out into an open boggy area with frozen mounds of cranberry bushes, marsh grass and gray, dead balsams.

His pace never varied, he forged on, head straight front as if unconcerned. However, his dark eyes were mobile, probing back and forth across the bog. There, to his left, concealed in those swamp balsams next to the high ground, a glimpse of orange?

"Hey, there," he called, his voice an unnatural intrusion on the silent world of white. He pivoted and headed directly toward the wall of trees, but the orange disappeared. . . . Or perhaps not there at all, he thought, maybe just his imagination.

A swamp creek blocked his path. It was frozen, but how solidly he couldn't be sure. Perhaps the man had crossed the stream further down, found a good-sized log. Norm worked his way through the bumpy mounds of grass beside the creek, moving upstream away from the small swamp lake the stream fed, eventually settling on a small log as his best chance and edging across on that, moving sideways, watching his feet. In midstream he glanced up to see the figure in orange behind the same screen of balsams, the barrel of a rifle poking out through the limbs. He stared. This time there could be no mistake.

Norm grunted, the fear and surprise breaking his concentration, his balance thrown off the narrow log. His foot slid sideways, smashing through the slush ice and dumping him into the freezing creek, his rifle dropping away. He lay there, chest-deep in murky swamp water, his elbows gripping at the edge of the ice for support, the freezing water soaking in against his flesh and inside his boots, the weight growing, dragging at his body. He glanced up, fifty yards away, at the head and shoulders of a man partially screened by brush, the face concealed behind the black bore of a rifle pointed directly at Norm's face.

CHAPTER III

The man was a dentist. His hands were small, pink, the fingers short, the fingernails well-manicured. His right forefinger touched the curved metal face of the trigger, taking up the slack. His face, a medium, handsome face, lightly tanned, balding on top, was without expression. He swung the rifle to center the scope on Norm as the big man lay chest-deep in the swamp creek.

All day long he'd been out here, poking along the edge of the seven-mile swamp, staring out at the tangles of tag alders and the carpet of snow, one part of the swamp looking exactly like the other. Hour after hour with the trees and the brush and the snow and not one sign of life. All that time and not a sound. No wonder his head had begun to hurt. But then he saw movement and, using his scope simply to look and see who it was, Norm, with his damnable capacity for imagining, jumped to conclusions.

He closed his eyes, recalling the first thing he ever shot to death, a blackbird with an orange stripe on its wing. "See if you can hit that bird," Glenn Sr. said to his ten-year-old boy, Glenn Jr. "Be steady, be steady," Glenn Sr. said, his hand resting on his boy's thin shoulders. "Just keep the bead and vee lined up like I said. And squeeze."

The .22 popped and the little blackbird crumpled and fell to the earth. "Hey, thataboy," Glenn Sr. said, tousling his boy's auburn hair. "Thataboy," he repeated as he took the rifle away, a safety measure so that Glenn Jr. couldn't possibly be hurt. "C'm'on. Let's go see if we can get another one."

Ten years old and Glenn Jr. had never been seriously hurt, scarcely even a bump or a bruise. He was the fourth child, the first boy after three girls. Glenn Sr., an official for the Illinois Department of Transportation, had been elated. "I was scared as hell you'd let me down again," he'd told his wife cheerfully as he held the six-and-a-half-pound boy. "Looks just like me, doesn't he?" he said, his thin face smiling from behind his thick glasses. "He's gonna be a doctor," he said on that first day of Glenn's life.

The two were inseparable, weekends, week nights, the closest of companions. Glenn Sr. got time off from work to take the boy to his first day of school, reluctantly entrusting him to the teacher, pointing out firmly that Glenn should be watched over carefully, "or else."

And during the last two weeks of July every summer of Glenn's childhood, Glenn Sr. packed up his travel trailer, his wife and three daughters, and with Glenn Jr. seated beside him for the whole long drive took the family to northern Wisconsin for a stay in a crowded campground and some unsuccessful father-and-son fishing.

The trips were usually uneventful, except for one, when Glenn, four years old and wearing his bulky lifejacket, wandered down to the lake all alone and played in the sand at the edge of the water until his father found him. "Goddamnit, I asked you to keep an eye on him," Glenn Sr. screamed at his wife, his hand still stinging from slapping her face, the one time he ever struck her. "He could have drowned."

Glenn Jr. didn't drown, and he didn't play football, or basketball, or baseball, or any team sports in which someone else was in control, in which he could easily be injured. In fact there were few times like the time when six-year-old Glenn managed to creep outside and was playing with two boys in a mud puddle down on the street corner, making tiny mud balls and tossing them at each other's back, running and squealing and laughing as they ran back and forth pelting at each other.

"Glenn, get up here," Glenn Sr. suddenly called from his driveway. "I told you not to play with those kids," Glenn Sr. said and sent the boy to take a bath and then to his bedroom where Glenn Jr. sat down in the center of his blue shag carpeting, his brown eyes wide, gazing at the blue flowered paper of his walls, and the blue bedspread and the blue curtains on the window. Hour after hour after hour he sat there un- moving, his toys stacked neatly in the nearby closet, the silence so deep and loud that his head began to hurt. And still he sat there.

"Keep Glenn out of the street and away from those Anderson kids," Glenn Sr. instructed his wife. "They're welfare, a bunch of rabble-rousers that'll get him hurt. Glenny doesn't need friends like that."

What Glenny needed was a good education, his fa- ther said. And he received it—high school, dental school, the entire ride carefully planned for and saved for. Glenn Jr. was thankful, even managing a smile as he stood beside his father on graduation day, peering into the camera at posterity, a chance to hang on his father's wall until dead.

And then, as Glenn Sr. should have known would happen but had never paused to consider, Glenn Jr. went off on his own, building up a dental practice, marrying one of his dental assistants, Barbara, and raising two children, Rachel and Glenn III, in their eighty-thousand-dollar suburban home in Des Plaines. Summers they went camping up north, once taking a longer trip out west to Yellowstone. The years passed.

Sunday night. The kids were in bed early in order to be ready for school the next day. Glenn lay on top of Barbara, her hands making their usual little circles on his back. Thrust, thrust, thrust, a hard driving with no feeling down below. "Glenn!" Barbara complained at his sudden violence. He rolled away, sweating. "What's wrong with you?" she asked. "You were hurting me."

"I'm sorry," Glenn said and rolled away, his legs pulled up to his chest as he willed himself to sleep.

The next day, to make up for his brief lack of control, he called Barbara from work. "Why don't we take the kids out for dinner tonight," he said. "We can go down to Kentucky Fried, then over to Bridgeman's for a malt."

"That sounds nice," Barbara said, and all was forgiven.

Just like—after the necessary twenty-four hours of stony silence—all was forgiven when he'd been on his once-or-twice-a-year drunk at a cocktail party. "But I never said or did anything wrong," he'd argue, truthfully enough, to Barbara. But the silent twenty-four-hour pout still held, one of the rules.

He'd been the model of a behaved drunk, standing there, quiet, a drink in hand, as he weaved slightly and listened to the talk. Like that of a fellow dentist, Peter Boyken, a sky diver.

"Dammit, I tell you, man," Peter said in his eager voice, "other than sex," here he winked, "it's the only thrill I get in life. I mean, you can only look in so many mouths, and what's new to see?" Peter waved his hands, spilling his Manhattan. Glenn stared. "I think

the human animal was born to danger," Peter continued. "It's part of his being. But now, look at us, survival insured, up and down the line. But fall out of
an airplane for two miles. Now that's living. Hell,
that's why we really have wars—to generate a little excitement, to feel alive again. Do you know what I
mean?"

Glenn looked unmoved. "It sounds a little far-
fetched," he mumbled.

Peter's eyes bugged outward. "Yeah, to you it
would be, Glenn. I mean, what have you ever, ever
done in your life that could really be called dangerous or exciting?"

Glenn shrugged.

"That's what I thought. You don't even know what
it feels like," Peter said, frustrated at Glenn's lack of
understanding. He turned on his heel, spilling more
of his drink, and walked away, unaware of the imaginary scope and crosshairs Glenn had centered on his
back. Just the slightest touch of the trigger, the
slightest movement. Glenn smiled, his lips barely
moving, the quivering inside violent, almost uncontrollable. . . .

But now, as he peered at Norm lying in the stream,
head and elbows on the edge of the ice, the control
was his completely.

The big man had figured it out, Glenn decided.
Why else did he keep coming? Two or three miles the
guy had tracked him. The thought provoked him.
One shot and Norm would slip away into the river,
carried away by the current. If it snowed before they
found Norm's tracks, they wouldn't find the body until spring. And then who could they suspect? Everyone? Another stray shot, the ballistic evidence, if any,
gone when he once again went to his distant gun-
smith and bought a new barrel. There'd be nothing.

Norm was struggling, trying to crawl out of the icy

hole. Glenn tightened up, the scope centered on Norm's rough, homely face, the curved trigger cold beneath his forefinger. "No," he thought, stopping himself as Norm looked back at him. But the rifle accidentally exploded.

The picture jumped. Glenn's innards contracted and short gasps of breath escaped him. He ventured forward a few steps, peering over the swamp grass at the hole in the ice and the sheen of black, slowly moving water. Still panting, he watched over the waving grass to make certain Norm hadn't simply ducked down in the water. Then he turned and crashed back into the forest, eyes gleaming, mouth wide with hilarity as he broke into a run through the snow and trees, rifle leveled. It bucked, the shock jolting up into his shoulders. He leaped a snow-covered log, rifle again leveled at an imaginary target off to one side. The powerful recoil again jolted the muscles of his arms, the thunder reverberated in his skull. Breathing, sweating, laughing, shooting.

He tripped and sprawled headlong into the snow, burying his rifle and face in it, giggling. He rolled on his back to face the sky, his head and face dusted with white, his chest heaving as he fought for air.

"Oh, Jesus. Face to face and I did it. Face to face."

After a few minutes the heaving subsided and he stood and brushed off the snow—the dentist once more. "Control, Glenn Jr.," he said quietly.

He checked the area. The wind blew gently, stirring the marsh grass. Clouds still raced across the blue sky, the snow sparkling under the beat of a cold sun, the scrub trees of the frozen swamp standing silently, the witnesses. And in the murky waters of the swamp creek Norm Petrie no doubt bounced silently along under the ice, his face white, the eyes open, at long last in his final resting place.

Glenn turned and made for the shack, circling

twice to confuse his trail, even getting lucky and shooting an eight-point buck on the way in. It all looked good, clean. He walked on in, dragging the buck, a quiet man in complete control.

CHAPTER IV

As he struggled in the water, Norm spotted the scope, the dim outline of the man, and the face hidden behind the black bore of the rifle. Instinctively, with a quickness belying his size, he slipped backward into the hole. As he sank into the dark freezing water, something, a bullet he figured, smacked the ice or water over his head. A death thought constricted his chest. He struck out, forging underwater downstream, heading the twenty feet away to a bend, clothes and boots dragging him down, a frenzy of sluggish motion, floundering and kicking in mud and water, rising up to hit ice, eyes open, blurred, clogged by a murky brown through which he could barely see light. His lungs ached. He cursed his panic and struck out again, this time with a strong breaststroke and frog kick. Two, three, good strokes, moving, moving, through an icy black grave from which he could never rise. Something stabbed into his face and he rolled in agony, lungs bursting, reaching up at the hard bottom of ice, the light more distinct up here, a world out there. But he couldn't push through. His lungs heaved, sucking at his throat and mouth, willing them to open for a breath of air, a breath of water, whatever was out there the lungs would accept. Just so the agony ended.

He moved backward, toward what he assumed was the middle of the stream, his feet feeling something solid like a submerged log. Back hunched, he pushed upward and popped neatly through a thin sheet of slush ice.

Air, pure, fresh air, a deep pain pouring into his starved lungs. So good, so sweet.

But with his joy Norm sobered, his mind clear. The grass rustled, a distinct crunching in the snow. He sank back into his icy coffin, only his face above water. There, through the marsh grass, the barest outline of a man peering out toward the stream. A slight turn and one or two steps and the man could see. The body turned, directly toward Norm.

Norm sank away, squatting in the black, icy water, and the pain gripped his chest again almost instantly. To struggle, to make a blind swim like that under the ice in water as black as his hair, to escape, and then to be gunned down like a helpless seal rising to an air hole.

His screaming lungs finally drove him to surface. His face was so numb from cold that he could only hope his mouth would open on its own. He poked only his face into the air and sucked quietly. His eyes swept the area. The tan marsh grass rustled softly, pushed by a gentle breeze, and the man was gone. A raven winged past, rustling the air, croaking its guttural cry as it searched for a carcass. Norm stood upright, the black water just below his chest. He shivered violently. Carefully, quietly, he broke off a few chunks of ice between him and the shore, working into thicker ice, then crawling up on that, easing himself out of the water and in tight to the shore. Cautiously he rose to his knees and peered across the swamp. He could see no one.

Up the shore, a matter of twenty feet, he could see

the log and the black hole where he'd crashed through. In the snow nearby his rifle lay, a magnet. Breathing gently, his eyes still flicking systematically over the area, he crept down through the grass and reached out and seized his rifle, hugging it close to the ice already forming on his jacket just like he'd hugged Jeffrey those years ago when little Jeffrey had stepped into water over his head up at the lake. One mouthful of water and Norm had picked him up, holding him close while the frail lad choked away his tears. And now Norm had his own protector, had his chance.

A violent shivering racked his body, bending him over in the ten-degree air. One thing, he had matches, wrapped and taped in a tin bouillon can, a safety margin he'd carried every year for thirty-three years of hunting. But with the cold and the wind and the long walk back to the shack would a fire do him any good? It'd take hours to dry his thick woolen pants and jacket. Hours. How many minutes could a soaked hunter stay alive out here? . . .

A rifle shot sounded in the woods across the creek, then a second one. "Move," he muttered, a selection of priorities. He stood straight and began a shuffling trot through the swamp, the agony of his innards as if he was being watched. He headed directly away from where he'd last seen the man, moving quickly into a stand of balsams that gave him cover and through that to the high land, eventually settling on building his fire beside a large dead poplar so he'd have plenty of firewood.

In minutes, using birch bark for kindling, he had a huge fire going and began to strip, hanging his jacket and shirt near the flames, taking off his boots and socks and standing on a tiny raft of logs tight against the flames, rifle nearby, eyes on the forest, arms wide open to the searing heat. He was a large figure, squatting there in his bare feet and red-and-black-checked hunting pants and white underwear top, his face rough, thoughtful as he watched the forest and turned his clothes, the bruise from the run-in with the underwater stick marring one cheek, his black hair matted from the stream. Outwardly he appeared calm, his face placid, like the flat surface of a lake on a windless day. And yet he'd almost died.

Trapped there, chest-deep in icy water, his rifle out of reach, helpless—and then a man dared shoot at him. He breathed softly, blowing outward.

One thing, death had loomed before and he'd acted as he should. But a sense of pride and relief couldn't still the question of how or why something like this could happen in the first place. A stranger, some crazy, passing through?

And there was the matter of the girl who had been killed the season before down by Coon Forks, in an area they'd been hunting in. And another hunter two years before that, down by the old pothole swamp they sometimes hunted. Only that body wasn't discovered until a week after the season ended. And then no one noticed. He should have remembered earlier.

One of the others? The very thought boggled him. Impossible. They'd all been together forever. Butch and Rod had hunted with him when they were teenagers in high school. And the others had been here almost as long. Go to the police, and that would be it, he thought. Go to the police.

But could he?

After an hour the nearby wood began to run short and Norm grimly pulled on his damp steaming socks and boots, his movements slow, deliberate, his eyes constantly turned to the surrounding forest, his head cocked whenever distant gunfire rattled through the woods. His woolen hunting clothes were still heavy with water but, for the moment at least, warm from the fire. He dressed slowly, as if filled with a deep sadness, then hefted his rifle, checking to see that the bolt had not frozen and that he still had a round chambered. Satisfied that things were the best they could be, he kicked snow over the fire and stomped it completely out, then set off toward the shack, his movements steady, slightly tensed as if coiled for action.

It was on the way back, just at the broad junction where the long highland finger they'd been on joined with the mainland, that he saw the tracks in the snow, fresh tracks coming back off the finger jutting into the swamp, tracks that joined with the others on the main trail that led from the shack, tracks heading directly back toward the shack.

For several minutes Norm did not move. His clothes were freezing up, caked with ice crystals, the legs of his pants and arms of his jacket stiff as if made of cardboard. He took off one stiffened mitten and rubbed at his ears, an effort at restoring circulation. "Better move," he said aloud, his eyes fixed on the tracks. "Better move."

He stumbled forward, his head on fire from exposure and anxiety, trying through the din to compose his story to the police. "A man pointed a rifle at me, and then he took a shot at me," Norm heard himself saying. "I dropped back through the ice and swam downstream under it and came up where he couldn't see me."

They'd smile, those fat little small-town rejects, and look at each other, nodding their heads. "Did you see what the man looked like or where he went?"

"No. He was too far away, too far back in the brush. I'm almost positive he returned toward our shack, though."

"Oh?" They exchanged glances. "You think he's one of your buddies in the shack then? Which one?"

"I don't know," Norm muttered. "I just don't know."

"You don't have any evidence whatsoever who it was?" they asked, taking him by the arm.

"I don't know, dammit . . . now I told you all I know so you do what you want. Just leave me alone." But they wouldn't, Norm knew, shaking his head back and forth, trying to lose his mountain of a headache the way a dog shakes off a flea.

He was moving steadily through the forest, eyes constantly probing, ears cocked, his stumbling gait like that of an escaped prisoner with chains on his ankles, a desperate effort to maintain some circulation in his feet and limbs. On the outside his clothes were frozen solid, slowing his movements, the ice on the legs making a maddening swish, swish, swish as they brushed together. In his condition he was surprised he even spotted the deer when, during a brief halt to catch his breath, a hint of movement attracted his attention. The bottoms of gray-brown legs were silently creeping down the steep ridge to his right. A deer. Now.

Norm straightened, about to resume his journey, when the deer crossed into a small opening in the trees, an alley. Norm held his breath, dimly aware that his heart was beating faster, dimly aware of the cold working toward his heart. It was a huge buck, as big as any he'd ever shot. Not the legendary big black he'd seen twice—the one Rod always swore he'd get— but a record nevertheless.

Norm waited, ignoring the logic that told him he must keep moving or die, tensing, watching the shadow of the buck, the towering rack of antlers, the glimpse of legs and part of a body, seeing the six-foot opening the buck must cross. "Take him," Norm thought, aware of the record, of the impression it would make on the others.

The buck stepped into the opening and paused, turning its rack toward Norm, the huge brown eyes wide, blind to the bright reds of Norm's jacket, pondering the strange, motionless form a hundred feet away. Norm stood stiff, arms frozen more by cold than from any attempt at stealth. He closed his eyes and winced. "Go, boy," he said in a hoarse voice, and waved awkwardly to shoo the deer away.

The buck's eyes widened. It seemed to crouch for a split second, muscles bunched, then abruptly exploded in one twenty-foot jump, then another, the white flag of its tail flashing once and disappearing into the forest.

The woods exploded with gunfire. "No," Norm gasped. He clawed his way forward through some brush, running, falling, picking himself up, panting and crashing on. He broke out into the open and saw the buck a hundred yards away. Obviously wounded, it had taken refuge behind a deadfall. In the time Norm took to blink, the deer jumped up and started dragging itself forward on its front legs, its once powerful hindquarters crippled and dragging uselessly. Norm snapped his rifle stiffly to his shoulder. . . .

"No, no, no, he's mine. He's mine," Rod wailed across the forest in a high pitch. He ran across an opening between Norm and the deer, fumbling with his rifle. The buck lunged away, its sleek muscles bulging, the air white with billows of its breath, the huge antlers waving from side to side as it spent every effort to escape.

Rod got off his shot. The deer flopped sideways, then struggled to its feet again and clawed forward on its front legs toward the sanctuary of the swamp. He shot again. Snow blew at its feet and it pulled harder, eyes bulging, breath billowing white clouds, blood flowing from its mouth. Another shot. It flopped sideways in the snow.

"I got it. I got it." Rod whooped. "Son of a bitch, I got it! Will you look at that! Wheee!"

"Finish him off," Norm yelled in a rage, shuffling

hurriedly toward the deer which had raised its head and was struggling to get up and run one last time.

"He's dead," Rod protested.

From fifty yards away Norm's shot smashed through the head of the buck and it lay still.

"Ya bastard, what'd ya do that for?" Rod yelled. "Ya wanna ruin my trophy? Christ!" He ran through the foot-deep drifts toward the buck, waving his rifle over his head. "I *got* that son of a bitch. I got him, goddamnit." He slid to his knees beside the buck's head, his eyes wide. He touched the thick antlers, counting the long white tines. "Fourteen points. Fourteen." He looked up at Norm, his small pug face wide with a grin, eyes glazed for the moment unable to focus. He was a small wiry man, his hair blond, curly, his face boyishly handsome with dark blue eyes that looked at a point just to one side of a person's head.

"Well, Norm," Rod said in his cocky tone, "I guess this puts you over the hill once and for all. The biggest rack you have in that shack is that twelve-pointer you killed up on the ridge. And that was over ten years ago. No one will ever beat this one. This big black is the biggest buck for a hundred miles around." Rod nudged at the huge buck with his toe, a gesture of triumph, but also of disbelief, as if frightened that somehow he'd be robbed of this measure of his success. He bent down and caressed the antlers. He glanced up at Norm and his grin disappeared. "The bastard's one hundred percent mine. He was dead. You didn't need to shoot that last shot."

"He's yours," Norm whispered.

"You're damn right he's mine. What the fuck happened to you?" Rod acted as if he'd just noticed Norm's frozen clothes, wet hair and stiff stance. "Ya fall in the fucking creek?" He laughed. "That's great. Norm Petrie, the big warrior, the great outdoorsman, falls through the ice in the creek. Jesus Christ, Norm, even Bernie knows the ice in that creek isn't safe, even in the dead of winter." He paused and looked up. "You fell in, didn't you?"

Norm shrugged, a sign of affirmation that started Rod howling again. And no hint of surprise that he stood here, Norm observed. He's keeping awfully cool if . . .

Painfully Norm bent down beside the huge buck as if in slow motion and buried his numb hands in the fur next to the warm flesh. Then he helped Rod wrestle the deer onto its back and stood shuffling back and forth, moaning silently to himself, waiting there freezing while Rod, oblivious to his damp clothes, gutted the animal. And still not one telltale hint of surprise from him.

The cleaning completed, they each took hold of a side of the huge rack and started through the forest, the heavy body sliding fairly easily on the snow, the flesh jiggling as the body slid up over logs, drops of blood falling from the open belly, the furrow of its passing marked in the snow. They dragged steadily, Rod chattering all the time, the work bringing life back to Norm's limbs. They reached the shack just before dark.

The others were all there, all outside helping to hang Glenn's eight-point buck up on the hanging pole beside David's spike buck. They turned as Norm and Rod approached, all eyes fixed on the fourteen-point buck. As if stiff-legged with shock, they shuffled forward.

"Son of a bitch," Butch said. "Look at the size of that thing. That yours, Norm?"

"He's mine," Rod yelled indignantly. "Norm doesn't get everything around here. This is the biggest buck this shack has ever seen. Besides, if Norm's top gun why hasn't he shot a buck for over three years?"

"Where'd you get him?" Merald asked. They

crowded around, drinks in hand, looking down on the huge gray-brown body.

"Only about a quarter mile back," Rod said. "Got him on the dead run. You should have seen him, nothing but horns coming through that woods. Horns and more horns. And here he is, dead, the goddamn legendary big black."

Norm, aware of Rod's lie, said nothing.

"What'd *you* see this aft, Norm?" Butch asked.

Rod laughed and blurted, "The bottom of the creek. The great woodsman fell through the ice on the creek."

The others turned in the dusk, for the first time noticing Norm's shivering and the ice-caked clothes. They stared him up and down, the looks amused, but not one of them acting out of the ordinary as far as Norm could see.

"You're the one always warning us about the creek ice being soft," Butch laughed. "How the hell did you manage to fall in yourself?"

"Someone chased me," Norm said, a nervous tremor making his voice rattle.

"Wooeee," they all laughed, roaring half at Norm's joke and half at his embarrassment.

"Let's get this thing hung up," Butch said, turning to Rod's deer.

Norm stared, as the subject of his wet clothes was laughed at and dropped. He'd almost died out there. Somewhere nearby was a killer and these guys laughed, but try as he might he could not bring himself to interrupt their enthusiastic chatter. He was shivering, he was exhausted, he needed to try to run it through his mind again, more clearly. . . .

"Grab ahold here," Butch called to Glenn, who stood silently off to one side with his rifle held cross arms. "Well, come *on,* put that fucking rifle down and lend a hand." He seized one antler as Glenn, carefully not looking at Norm, bent to seize the other.

"I'd say we've had one damn successful opening day and deserve a drink or two," Butch continued. "Three bucks out of six guys isn't bad. I've got a feeling this is going to be one of the best seasons we've ever had around this shack."

"The best season," Rod said, "the best season ever."

CHAPTER V

The others lay around the hunting shack. They were sweating, red from the exertion of the first day in the wilds and the run of raw liquor down their throats. They were crowded in, the smell of damp bodies mixed with the thick heat from a blazing fireplace and a turned-up furnace. Mounds of soiled winter clothing, thermal underwear, wool socks, blaze-orange coats and belts holding long hunting knives hung from the rafters where sets of antlers from years gone by clogged the airspace. They lounged easily, tired city legs stretched out before them, belts unbuckled, stomachs spread wide, cold drinks in their hands, Glenn off to one side casually cleaning his rifle, Norm in the kitchen, as usual doing Bernie's job and preparing supper. Occasionally loud horse-laughs sounded. Eyes glinted. The smell of a thick roast and fresh venison tenderloin carried from the kitchen. A bottle made the rounds. They sank into themselves. Butch farted.

The hunting shack had been built down at the end of what had once been a twenty-mile length of near impassable logging road, a road that had, over the years, been gradually chewed down to two miles off of

THE HUNTING SHACK 43

the nearest gravel road. It was a dull, dark-brown log cabin that at first glance could have been an abandoned logging shack from the turn of the century when thousands of two-legged animals invaded the silent beauty of the towering virgin timber, timber they casually assumed to be endless. The shack, situated on the solid ground between a high ridge and a balsam swamp, blended so well with the dark green of the surrounding spruce that it was easy to be almost upon it before seeing it.

At the time young Norm had helped to build the cabin, it was a crude pioneer affair with four walls and little else, made with their own hands, using materials supplied by the forest, as Norm often recalled to the others. Over the years the shack evolved considerably: the dirt floor was replaced with cement, two more bunkrooms were added, a rock fireplace built, large thermopane picture windows were set into the logs and, as civilization made its inroads, electricity and running water and a bathroom were added. What had once been a spare, single-room log cabin became cluttered with kitchen appliances, a small bar, carpeting, and used storebought furniture mixed incongruously with the primitive, heavy pieces handmade by their forefathers.

Still, the pretense of the past remained. The log rafters were lined with dozens of sets of odd-shaped, variously colored and mounted antlers. Each set carried its own story, some of them all but forgotten and their participants dead, some of them embellished into legend, some into retold tales of foulups and miscalculation. . . .

As on this day, Glenn thought, the cold shock of Norm's return still with him, a quivering deep in his guts, the thought there that the others might actually find him out.

What the hell was Norm waiting for? He must know who did it.

Glenn closed his eyes. . . . He was sitting down at the supper table with Barbara and Rachel and Glenn III. Barbara said the prayer, the conviction firm in her tone, and they ate, Barbara watching Glenn III and Rachel, correcting them when necessary, speaking of school and grades, Glenn nodding fatherly support. . . . After supper into the living room to watch the news on TV, sitting in his lazy-chair with his cup of hot coffee, one dollop of cream, one sugar. The news over, rising and picking up the athletic bag Barbara had packed and going into the kitchen where she was finishing the dishes.

"Leaving now?"

"Yes," kissing her on the forehead. "See you in a couple of hours."

"Have a good run," she said as he went out the kitchen door.

And he did, three miles, forty-eight times around the banked wooden track, his concentration complete, watching for the gray beam with the yellow line, adding it to his total each time he passed, watching the red second hand on the wall clock, figuring his lap time, going faster and faster, sweat flowing, spittle drying on his lips, finishing with nothing left. Then shower, then home to sit with Barbara while she sewed and he watched the ten o'clock news, then off to bed where he curled into his little ball and willed himself to sleep.

In the morning to work. "Good morning," he'd say in his pleasant, mild tone to his two dental assistants, Nancy and Mildred. Nice girls, kept his schedule filled, cleaned his instruments, kept them laid out in the exact order prescribed. People came in and he looked at their record cards outside the doorway, then greeted them with their first names. "Hi," he said, and peered into the open mouth.

And at 5:30 he finished and went home.

A good life, Glenn argued, unaccustomed tears in

his eyes, the first since childhood. He got up now from his chair in the corner, away from the big fireplace, and with his face turned away from the others made his way to the bathroom, locking himself in. He bent over the stool, cramped, retching as quietly as he could, mucus streaming from his nose and mouth. He stood up and stared into the mirror at his red eyes and the slime on his chin and upper lip. "I'm all right," he mumbled in a weak voice, talking to the two of them. He picked up a bar of soap and began to lather his face, washing it clean, looking into the mirror, then washing it again. . . . There'd been that one night at home when Barbara had gone with Rachel and Glenn III for their swimming lesson and he'd been sitting there in the silent house in front of the silent television. For two hours he'd sat quietly, brown eyes alert, flicking back and forth over the dark paneling and the bookshelves and the television screen. In the kitchen the refrigerator clicked on, and sometime later, off. A car passed out front. A dog barked. He sat still, his eyes shifting around and around the room. After two hours he got up and walked into his den and took his deer rifle from the closet, caressing the smooth satin finish, holding it to his cheek. The hollow feeling in his guts vanished. Abruptly, in the stillness of his own house, forty-year-old Glenn Jr. crouched, his brown eyes slits. He crept to the doorway, peeking out into the living room, seeing the way was clear, suddenly moving forward and diving behind the sofa.

Calm, with deliberation, breath held in careful check, he poked the rifle over the end of the red-and-black flowered sofa, sighting down the hallway toward the bedrooms. There. He saw them ducking away. He steeled himself, a spring coiling, suddenly shooting upward and tearing across the room to the end of the hallway. He flattened himself against the wall, wait-

ing, then abruptly whirled out into the hall, rifle at
the ready. They were gone.

He crept slowly down the hallway, crouched, the
rifle held before him for instant action. He moved
into the yellow-flowered world of Rachel's bedroom,
rifle leveled, spraying them as they crouched in the
closet. "Pow, pow, pow," he said quietly through his
heavy breathing. *Kablam,* and the rifle jumped. The
steel-jacketed bullet ripped through Rachel's closet,
through two dresses, and through the wall into Glenn
III's room where it cut a deep furrow in the dresser
and lodged in the wallboard beneath the window
. . . He'd been cleaning the rifle and it went off,
he told Barbara later, but she never understood what
he'd been doing in Rachel's room, or why the rifle
had been loaded in the first place, a subject she and
Glenn Sr., when he was around, stayed with for
months. . . .

Glenn stared at his now clean face in the bathroom
mirror of the shack, wincing from his stomach
cramps. In the outer room the ignorant banter of the
others continued. "Idiots," he muttered, keeping his
ear cocked for the sound of Norm's voice.

Norm? He felt for the Luger pistol he'd stuffed in
the belt under his red flannel shirt, an inanimate
piece of cold metal, the old German Schutzstaffel, SS,
styling the reason he'd bought it. As soon as Norm
spoke, he thought, working against the weakness in
his guts, as soon as he pointed the finger, he'd have to
move. Anything to cover himself. He knew they'd
want it that way. Even if he died too.

A typical Saturday night, and still not one hint of
surprise at his being here, Norm thought as he sur-
veyed the others one by one. He pictured them as
they stood or knelt in front of the three hanging deer
for their opening-day portrait, grubby-looking men
with their long underwear and suspenders and hunt-

ing jackets and rifles and drinks in hand, smiling at the camera as they arranged themselves around the three carcasses, a typical group of hunters, everything normal. Except he knew better, and so did one of them.

As usual on Saturday night, they began a poker game immediately after supper, drinking, still eating, nibbling on venison sausage and cheese and crackers. Norm wrapped the massive paw of his hand around the sweating glass of his drink, gazing one by one at the others, aware of the damp clothes and body odor and roaring fireplace and oil heater and kitchen smells and cigarette and cigar smoke and cooking grease, all tightly enclosed by the four walls of the log cabin. Abruptly he folded his cards, rose, his chair clattering backward as he boiled up over the table, his brown eyes squinting down at the others, blinking, fists clenched, his body encased by black, icy water, his back hunched upward, pushing against the icy roof of his coffin, his lungs crying for air, water, anything. He turned quickly toward the front door.

"Going to check out the stars, great hunter?" Butch said as Norm slammed the door behind him.

A little dizzy from his lack of oxygen, Norm stumbled away from the cabin and leaned against a tree. The cool, fresh night air of northern Wisconsin seared into his lungs, a knife of ecstasy that almost drove him to his knees. He closed his eyes and breathed deeply. After a time he lifted his head and contemplated the sky of stars. He shook his head, his mind clearing in the cold.

He glanced down the length of his long body, aware of the slackness of his gut so detested by the beautiful Joannie, a young woman ten years his junior. There were too many years between now and the days of the shining knight when he'd met her, incredibly, in that singles bar. There she was, a small town divorcée's daughter just escaped from high

school and home to the big city. And there stood big
Norman Petrie, also from a small town, but with
eight years in Chicago behind him and a fatherly
trustworthiness she seemed to need, that and a good
job and a twenty-thousand-dollar nest egg he'd been
saving up ever since high school. He'd still been solid
then, retaining the firmness of the all-conference tight
end. And he'd been reliable, something he'd always
prided himself on. But was it enough? Especially for
a girl like Joannie. Even then he couldn't have been
considered handsome.

He looked from his midriff to the stars. If she'd
seen him today, under the water, under the ice, not
panicking, a survivor . . .

The shack door opened and a shaft of light hit his
legs. Raucous laughter carried from inside. "Hey,
what're you doing out here?" Rod laughed, his handsome face and blond curls tossed back. He waded
sideways off the shoveled trail and began to urinate
in the snow. "You praying to your old medicine man
to speak to the Hunt God to makeum heap big medicine so you killum big buck?" Rod always liked to
twist the needle about Norm's quarter-breed Indian
blood.

Norm said nothing, deliberately turning and heading back to the thick gas of the cabin where the others had taken a break from the poker game to freshen
their drinks, relieve full bladders and grab for a
snack.

"Lotsa stars, eh, Norm?" Butch said, as Norm came
in and closed the door.

"Lotsa stars," Norm agreed.

They settled back in around the large round table
and resumed their poker. A typical Saturday night.

But Norm knew he couldn't let it be.

"There's something I'd like to say," Norm finally
brought himself to announce between hands, the ef-

THE HUNTING SHACK 49

fort of speaking as great as anything he'd ever done, almost as bad as trying to ask Joannie to marry him.

Butch gathered up the deck of cards and began to shuffle. "Well, what is it, Norman? You're moving to a new house again?"

The big construction boss laughed.

"Gotta move upwards," Merald said with a friendly chuckle. "What Joannie wants, Joannie gets. Just like all women."

"What the hell does that mean?" Bernie muttered in a thick voice. His eyes were watery, his large bumpy nose solid red, the ex-chef who now worked in a small tavern across from Norm's factory, the most recent of many jobs Norm had found for him since Bernie's divorce and abrupt decline afterward. "If Norm's got something important, let him say it."

"There have been two hunters killed by stray bullets in this general area in the last three years," Norm said, sweating now as he struggled past the banter. Why had he walked around all these hours, through supper, with this on his mind, scrutinizing the others closely, saying nothing?

"Two hunters?" Merald asked. Merald was a big man, soft and fat, a real estate developer with three shiny hunting rifles to select from. He looked at Norm through his rimless glasses, a fat cigar tucked in the corner of his mouth. "I don't recall two. There was that girl that was shot last year. We all heard about her. Who else was there?"

"We were," Norm said.

"Someone shoots in my direction they better make it good or I'll blow their fucking head off," Rod said, gathering in his cards. "There's getting to be too goddamn many hunters around here, anyhow."

"I remember that girl they found last year," Glenn said, voice casual. "That was down by Coon Forks. We were all in there the day before."

"The same day the authorities thought she was

killed," Norm said. "They didn't find her body until the following day."

"So what?" Merald asked. He glanced at Butch and shook his head, rolling his eyes toward the ceiling.

"Could be a coincidence," Glenn said easily. "We don't even know how close to the exact area any of us were."

"The paper said the Coon Forks road and the CC road," Norm said. "Exactly where we were at." Norm paused, seeing their shrugs. Somehow, despite the dryness of his throat, he managed to continue. "And the year before last, there was a guy killed in that swamp on the west side of Camp Nine hill. You may not have heard about him, but a logger came across his body about a week after season closed."

"You mean that open swamp with that thick island in the middle?" Merald asked as he slid a bet into the center of the table. "Open for a dollar."

"That's where I got that eight-pointer year before last," Rod said. "That son of a bitch was going full goddamn tilt across those cranberry bushes, thirty feet at a leap. One shot, *kablam,* folded right there. Hit 'em right in the eye. Did he ever fold."

"Yeah, but you were aiming for the fucking chest," Butch said. "Balls, talk about luck. And don't tell me you were aiming for the fucking head on a running deer."

"I at least *got* the son of a bitch . . . as I recall, you haven't got shit the last three years."

"Where the hell do you think the venison you're eating came from?"

"Yeah, from an illegal doe. Anybody can shoot a fucking doe. They just stand there and look at ya."

"Get fucked, Rodney," Butch said mildly. "We had a good meal. That's all that counts."

A good meal, Norm thought. But most of the deer lay out in the forest rotting, a fact he'd been witness to earlier that day, cutting over there after hearing

THE HUNTING SHACK 51

the loud, rapid fire—Butch, cutting down the forest again. What a maniac when he wrapped his huge hands around a gun. Shoot, shoot, shoot, like a sex nut with a hard on and no way to get it off. Slamming away at an illegal doe. When he approached, Norm found Butch elbow deep in the gray swirls of bloody intestines as he reached inside the steaming stomach cavity to rip away the tenderloins from inside the backbone. "Some fresh tenderloin and onions will really go good for supper tonight," Butch had said, but Norm had already walked away.

Norm shifted his long form and wiped at the sweat on his forehead, looking from Butch to the others, debating exactly how he should play this, how the men would react. "The thing is," he continued, raising his voice in an attempt to command attention, "they never discovered who shot those people, the guy or the girl."

"Maybe something's going on," Bernie mumbled. He sucked heavily at his drink, his eyelids dropping, thin shoulders hunched.

"The guy was three years ago, the girl last year," Butch said, ignoring Bernie. "A dozen or so people a year get killed in this state hunting. The law doesn't always figure out what happened. Balls, Norm, we talked about this last year when we heard the news. What's the big deal all of a sudden?"

"Fucking law around here couldn't catch someone if they saw them commit the crime," Merald said. "That fatass sheriff Bailey and his deputies do nothing but cruise around in their squad cars looking to hand out tickets."

"Hey there, deerslayer," Merald yelled at his son, David. "How about getting your old man a fresh drink here. Just because you shot a spike doesn't mean you can sit on your butt all night."

Norm watched the short pudgy boy move reluctantly to pour his father a drink. Fourteen years old

and the boy already had his first buck. . . . Norm
recalled that morning before dawn, two below zero,
and Bernie and young David trudging along behind
him in the dim light, heads lowered to follow his
steps. Once Norm paused and glanced toward the
outlines of the tops of the trees where the last of the
stars slowly receded into the white of a coming dawn.
He pulled young David to his side and quietly indi-
cated the way the outline of the trees on the high
ridge dipped down into a deep saddle, a natural
crossing place for deer, a good stand, close to the
shack, which Merald had always laid claim to.

They dropped Bernie off, and Norm took David
and posted him on a stand where he could watch the
open ridge flat where the ridge forked. David
breathed gently, tensed, recalling his father's instructions to listen to whatever Norm said. "Norm's as
good as any woodsman up in these parts," Merald
had told him. "For one thirteen-year stretch there he
shot a buck every year, sometimes two or three, once
five. You pay attention to him. . . ."

"You've got runways going in three directions,"
Norm had whispered softly so his voice wouldn't
carry. "Try not to shift around too much or turn
your head more than necessary. Look with your eyes.
Deer spot movement more quickly than you do. The
wind will be picking up shortly and it should be in
your face. That way nothing should smell you unless
the wind begins shifting a lot. I'll be back to check on
you in a couple of hours. Maybe I'll kick something
up. Stay here as long as you can. If you get too cold,
work back down the ridge to the first saddle. Your
dad will be there. All right?"

"Yes, sir," David whispered back.

Norm smiled to himself at David's fear. He recalled
Jeffrey's backhanded comment that David was a
loudmouthed bully at school. Jeffrey, his son. "He
can hunt when he's sixteen if he wants to. That's

soon enough," Joannie had said. But Norm new it'd be too late.

He'd left the young city boy alone then. And later, after hearing a flurry of wild shooting, he'd rushed back to see what had happened.

"Sonofabitching kid did all right," Merald had yelled as Norm approached the father and son and the dead yearling. "Fourteen years old. Not many kids that age can say they've killed a deer. No buck fever or nothing." David's grin almost covered his plump face.

"Not bad," Norm had murmured and bent down to feel at the young buck, aware of its life from minutes before. Aware that the boy was watching his work with the knife, he expertly slit into the belly, the warmth of the chest cavity steaming the air, the blood and guts of the fresh kill warm on his large hands. Merald had brushed his huge form beside him, grunting with the strain of bending down, dipping one finger into a pool of blood inside the cavity, then rising and smearing David's cheeks with the warm blood. "First kill, first blood," Merald said with solemn pride, a large cigar clamped firmly in the corner of his mouth. David stood straight, shoulders back, chest out, a happy grin on his fat, bloody face.

But David's buck, like Butch's doe, had been in the morning, seemingly weeks before the man had shot at him while he lay in the black river water. In the shack the banter of the card game continued—talk of the hunt, Rod's tenth story about the fourteen-pointer, talk of their jobs in the city, of their upcoming annual trip into Hurley on Sunday night and the prospect of seeing what new women worked at the taverns—and in the midst of it all Norm was aware that what he knew the others—except for one—did not. There was another breed of hunter among them.

"Today when I was out in the woods, I saw a guy

aiming his rifle at me," Norm said, still forcing his way into the talk.

"See your one and raise you two more," Butch said to Merald. He leaned sideways on his hams and cut a loud fart.

"What did he look like?" Bernie asked.

"I couldn't tell for sure. But when I ducked, and he saw that I'd spotted him, he ran. He ran like hell, I tell you. Like he was frightened."

The others finally paused, staring at Norm, judging how to take this. "What the hell would he do a thing like that for?" Merald asked.

"Embarrassed," Butch grunted as he displayed his winning cards and raked in the pot. "The son of a bitch was probably looking to see who you were, and when you saw him he took off. Didn't want you to know who was pointing a rifle at you. I know I'd be damn pissed if someone pointed a loaded rifle at me just to see who I was."

"I followed the guy's tracks," Norm continued. Why had he waited so long? "That's why I fell in the stream. The guy was aiming at me and I slipped off a log and broke through the ice." He glanced around at the eyes that were fixed on him. "The guy took a shot at me and I had to swim downstream under the ice to escape."

CHAPTER VI

The silence in the room throbbed, the thick, warm air choking. Norm's brown skin drew taut under the stares of the others. He glanced down at his weathered and callused hands, working hands with big bones and veins standing out on the hairy backs. One hand gripped his drink and he took a deep swallow, the ice clattering in the silence.

Butch began to chuckle quietly, his ample stomach shaking. "Oh, Norman, what are we going to do with you?" The others joined in, the laughter growing in volume, echoing off the walls, filling the room.

"But it's true."

"Come *on*, Norm," Rod said. He shook his blond curly hair, his blue eyes shining with amusement. "You can't be serious. Why the hell did you wait so long to tell us?"

Merald caught Butch's attention and rolled his eyes toward Norm, the real estate executive calling a crazy man to reason. "Norman. Norman. What the hell are you doing?" He laughed as if nervous, Norm thought. "Christ almighty, all the things I've done, all the people I've met, from bums to congressmen and governors, all types, and never have I met anyone with an imagination as . . . wild as yours. You're not serious about this, are you?"

Norm nodded, his rugged face solemn.

"Son of a bitch," Rod said, shaking his head and smiling. "We *know* you fell through the ice, Norm. Why don't you just say you were stupid enough to walk on it instead of making up these tall tales. What is this, a tall-tale contest? Maybe you got too much water on the brain and it froze your mind."

Norm shrugged.

"I think he's serious," Merald said.

Norm nodded.

"And you think the man who shot at you is the same man who killed that girl last year, and that other guy?"

Norm nodded.

"Aw, son of a bitch!" Butch exploded to his feet, almost knocking over the large round table. His huge form towered over them, his heavy cheeks bright red. He pointed a stubby finger at Norm's face. "Get hold of yourself, pardner," he said in a suprisingly soft voice. "I ain't really interested in this kind of fairy tale bullshit. Now if you're up for making up tales, you're going about it all wrong."

Bernie stood, wavering slightly, shaking his finger as if to caution the others. "You guys better listen. I think Norm's serious about this. Aren't you, Norm?"

"Goddamnit, Bernie, why don't you lay off that bottle," Merald snapped.

"I have as much right to have a drink now and then as you do." Bernie's voice was shrill. The dozens of antlers that hung in the rafters were silent onlookers.

"Easy, Bern," Norm said and put a hand on Bernie's shoulder.

As the exchanges went on, Glenn quietly moved over to the chair piled with clothes. He reached behind and touched the smooth stock of his loaded rifle, also aware of the comforting lump of the Luger tight against his flat stomach. As he watched the others' reactions, and Norm's struggle, a memory frame clicked and held. . . . He thought of himself with Barbara just after their Sunday night sex, the deed done, he figured as he rolled away and she murmured her weekly lie about how good he'd been, her moans and movements exactly like the week before. "Honey," he said into the dark, "I should tell you that during the last few years I've been going up north hunting, I've been shooting hunters out in the forest."

Silence.

"Just one a year," he explained patiently. "No one knows. They find the guy, and with no signs or readable tracks they figure the guy was hit by a stray bullet. And I always do it when we hunt away from the shack, each time in a different area, and only when there's a good chance of snow."

Silence, but Barbara was looking at him in the dark.

"I use steel-jacketed bullets so I figure the bullet goes right on through, but I still get rid of my rifle barrel afterward, file off the serial numbers and throw it in the river. I use an alias and buy a new one at different sporting shops around the state. No one knows."

"Glenn," she said in her quiet wail, her way of commanding him. *"What* are you talking about?"

"Shooting people. Just one a year, Barb. That's all. It's something, I'll tell you. I don't know what it's like taking dope, but this is really something." He smiled, reflecting. "Your old heart gets thrashing so hard you think it's going to bust your chest. And your mind. My god, Barb, your mind, it just sort of expands, tingles and then burns." He jerked his head from side to side.

"Glenn, stop this nonsense. . . ."

"And all I have to do is point my rifle and move my forefinger a quarter of an inch. A quarter of an inch. Can you get how simple that is? That's the beauty of it all. It's so damn simple. . . . Incidentally, do you think I should tell dad?"

"*Glenn*," Barbara wailed, sick and tired and indignant at being teased so crassly just because of her long-standing objections to his guns. A dumb stupid story, and she told him so. . . .

And the others in the shack were just like Barb, Glenn saw now. A tall tale. Things like that didn't happen in real life, at least not with people you knew. He almost smiled, but as he glanced at Norm, shivering briefly, seeing the big man purposely ignoring him, setting him up, he shifted the Luger under his shirt and sat forward, striving for a calm appearance, appraising Norm closely as if looking at a badly decayed molar, methodically contemplating the treatment. "Norm"—he coughed to clear his throat—"I've never seen you like this. We've been together in this shack for a long, long time. We know each other, trust each other. We know things have been rough on you at home. That puts on a lot of pressure. I'm not trying to accuse you or anything, but perhaps you might think about going in to see a psychiatrist."

"Hey, this *happened*," Norm said, his brown eyes direct. "I don't need the accusations—"

"But you're the one making the accusations," Glenn said, maintaining his customary, quiet, thoughtful manner.

Butch stepped to the kitchen counter and filled a water glass half full of whiskey. He shook his head, his face serious. "Glenn's right, Norm. This is goddamn insanity. I can't understand you. I used to figure you for being about as solid and reliable as they come. But this? How long have we been together in this shack, Norm? Figure it out. Twenty-five years? Good years. And now you come in here and actually suggest something like this. By all rights, Norm, we should smack you right in the mouth just for thinking it."

Bernie shook his head, squinting back and forth between Butch and Norm. He scratched at the side of his head. "Mmmmm, I dunno, Butch. Norm doesn't lie . . . . or tell stories."

Butch rolled his eyes toward the ceiling and nodded at Bernie. "Let's play some fucking cards. I don't like this getting upset. Just let things be. Your deal, Bernie."

"I'll shuffle," Merald said and started to gather up the deck.

"I can get it," Bernie muttered and made a grab, fumbling the deck from his hands and scattering cards on the floor.

"Give me the goddamn cards," Butch yelled. "And why don't you go to bed, Bernie?"

"Wha' da ya mean," Bernie protested. "I'm a'ri', can't a guy drop a deck a cards an'more?"

"Deal me out," Norm said and stood up. "I'll stoke the fire." He turned away, the others glancing at each other and nodding their heads at Norm's back. Was the big man going to simply forget his story about being shot at, they seemed to silently ask.

"Yeah, I'm out too," Glenn mumbled, clattering to his feet and running outside, hand to his mouth.

"Doc's sick again," Rod laughed, his voice echoing in the silence.

"It's the same every year," Merald said after a few seconds, attempting to break the silence. He glanced quickly at Butch as if seeking permission to speak. "If the bastard would practice up during the year, it wouldn't hit him so hard. He gets here and guzzles like hell for the first two days, and his system can't take it."

"If doc'd stand up to his old lady," Rod said, "it wouldn't be so hard on him. She won't allow a drop of liquor in that house and he won't stand against her. Ya gotta show 'em who's boss or you're finished. They'll nag ya to death."

The others said nothing, aware that Rod sometimes beat his wife and once put her in the hospital with internal bleeding, an incident that brought in the authorities. Sue had refused to press charges.

Merald stood up, and Butch asked, "Nobody's going to play?"

"I've had enough," Merald said. "We've got all week. I want some shuteye. That damn drive from Chicago still has me tired out."

"Well, son of a bitch," Butch said. "Norm, you and your wild-ass stories. I was winning, and now you busted up the game. What the hell did you make that shit up for, anyhow?"

"It's not made up," Norm said.

"Then why didn't you speak up earlier?" Glenn asked as he stomped back inside, wiping his mouth. "Damn, Norm, if this really happened I'd think you would have come back here screaming like hell. Pile into the jeep and go to the police. Something. It'd be the rational thing to do. At least not wait for half the night to pass." (His heart pounded like a triphammer.)

Norm shrugged. "I suppose it seemed too unreal. I was worried about the reaction, I figured some people might react like this."

The others stared, the silence deepening.

"Look," Butch said, "just for the joke of it let's go over this again, Norm. You saw a guy aiming a rifle at you. You went over there and saw where he ran. Then you followed him and saw him aiming at you again and fell through the ice. He took a shot—at least you think he might have—and you swam under the ice to escape? To where?"

"Twenty or thirty feet down around the bend. I pushed up through some slush ice and waited until the guy left. He came near me but I ducked back under the water until he left. I think he figured I drowned. On the way back I saw the tracks heading this way."

"You swam under the ice in that dirty swamp creek, then hid under the water?" Merald asked, his eyes slit behind his rimless glasses, the large cigar bobbing.

Rod laughed and clapped his hands. "I've never heard anything like this. Let's go tell the police. But I want to go along. I've gotta see their faces when they hear this one."

"They'll lock Norm up," Bernie said. He coughed, wheezing deeply to clear his throat.

Norm stared down at the others, the lines in his brown skin clean, sharp. The lines did not move as he spoke. "It happened," he said. "If you want, we can leave it at that and see what happens."

"It happened and now you want to leave it?" Rod said. "First you tell us you were shot at, now you tell us to leave it?"

"That's insane," Glenn said. "Pure and simple." He spoke softly, but his eyes, for anyone looking, were wide.

Butch pushed back from the table, stood and walked purposefully over to Norm. A large-boned man, well-muscled from his years in the construction trade in spite of the fat, he slowly, deliberately gripped the front of Norm's green-and-white flannel shirt, bunching up the cloth in his hands, pulling Norm close. "Norman, you're pissing me off. Something's happening with your mind. You should know that from what's been going on back home. Dammit, Norm, you're screwing up the mood of this shack, of the whole season." The black cave of Butch's mouth yawned at Norm's face. "Look at us." He jerked at Norm's shirt. "Look at us. Twenty-five years since we came here as boys with our old men. And now you start making up stories like this. It doesn't make sense, Norm. *None* of it."

Norm stared directly into Butch's small eyes, their faces inches apart. "It happened, Butch," Norm said in his low monotone. "I thought you guys deserved a warning. That's it."

Butch shoved Norm and he fell backward, catching his leg on the woodbox beside the fireplace and stumbling into the corner against the wall. He stayed there, looking silently up at Butch, saying nothing.

Butch glanced at the others, a deep silence among them, then back to Norm, who remained in the corner taking the measure of Butch's capacity for violence, for shooting an illegal doe, for shooting anything that moved. . . . Butch said, "Aw, fuck it. Let's get to bed."

"Yeah, let's get to bed," Merald echoed.

After the others had turned in, Norm stayed out in the living room, lying on the unfolded sofa in front of the blazing fireplace, his usual spot to spend the night.

One by one he thought of the others: David, Merald's kid, silent, frightened by all the shouting. Glenn, just as unworried as ever, scratch him. Same for Bernie, still desperate, still sucking too heavily on the booze, a friend. Then Rod, always pushing, like with his father-in-law's mobile home business—doubling the volume of business, he bragged, but losing money heavily, the word went—and with a real thing against Norm that seemed to run deeper than just the shack bag records . . . Merald, still growing, in girth as well as his business, and still seeking more. And Butch, the housing contractor, the classic straw boss, but who'd made no attempt to suppress at all his outburst against Norm that night, as far as Norm could see. . . .

Common men, ordinary men. One of them a killer?

Even now, the incident fresh in his mind, the black confusion of being trapped under the ice had become a permanent part of him. The rest of his life seemed all but erased, a dimly remembered past that had suddenly lost its meaning.

The question: did he draw the man out?

To actually be doing that, taking your own kind simply for the sake of killing. And never to show a sign? The unreality of it all boggled him. He'd expected more, the others incredulous but one man at least moving somehow to defend himself. But complete disinterest, disbelief? He shook his head. He'd sat on it too long after coming back, he could see that now. Hurt his credibility.

He closed his eyes, recalling the distant image across the swamp, the running tracks, circling, falling, and the little glimpse of orange behind the balsam across the creek. He couldn't even say for sure how big the man was.

The right thing—the only thing—would be to go to the police and let them come in and investigate. With the deaths from prior years, they'd have to get on it, wouldn't they? But he could still manage a smile in his slow, ponderous way, amusement at himself and at how Joannie would react, her taunts about his failure to run straight to the police. "Are you nuts?" she'd yell. He stared into the dancing flames of the fireplace, his dark eyes gleaming. Hard to figure . . . all of it. . . . Who could figure Kim, for example, and her giggling cheerleader friends. The world changing all around, and they still talked about boys and turning on, Joannie actually giving Kim birth control pills at age sixteen. And there was the beer party just this September, after a football game, fifteen- and sixteen-year-olds. And marijuana besides. Kim was there, the cops said. Although she didn't have any grass or do anything wrong, she'd yelled and stomped away.

"Get back here," he had commanded, but she hadn't even looked back. Helter skelter, running everywhere, no focus. . . .

All his life he'd tried to be disciplined. But not Joannie. "Let them breathe," she had said. "Let them just experience and learn best they can." But every rule said the young were taught the hazards of life by their parents. What was a man supposed to do?

Even with Jeffrey, his son, he could not figure it. . . . "No guns, no hunting," Joannie decreed. "Not until he's sixteen." And somehow, with no hunting together, and between work and the cocktail parties, Jeffrey, who came to hate the sports Norm loved, drifted away into his room with his collections of comics and science fiction books. Norm shook his head. Fifteen years old and comic books and science fiction. Was a man, a father, to say anything? He rubbed his face, at the tiredness he'd brought hundreds of miles north from Chicago. "It doesn't matter," he mumbled at a hundred rationalizations, thinking on the man in the swamp. Civilized behavior be damned. He'd see this through in his own way, like a man was supposed to. Period. Let them chew on that.

He sighed and settled down, glancing at the gaping black doorways to the two back bunkrooms, ancient caves in which the others lay staring at the dark. A tremor rippled the length of his back. Swam under the ice to escape. If only Joannie could have seen. And he became filled with a strange elation, a strange movement deep in his body. His nose wrinkled as if from a faint sour stench drifting from the back bunkrooms. Fear. Unmistakable fear. And he well knew how cunning and ferocious a cornered animal could be.

CHAPTER VII

A deep inner alarm brought Norm directly from sleep to awareness. He stared at the darkness, at the gray-white light from the front picture window. It was time.

He lay quietly, not moving. In the bunkroom with the snorers, Butch and Merald and Bernie buzzed away like the deep bass burp of bullfrogs on a hot summer night, the effects of last night's drink locking them in a stupor. Norm rose up on one elbow and glanced about, stomach rolling at the dark that stank with the sour odor of half-empty whiskey and beer glasses and stale cigarette smoke. . . .

Eventually, breakfast over, he stood in the gray light of the cabin and prepared for the coming day, taking a sandwich, bouillon cubes and a small tin can for melting snow for his noon meal, packing the items in a tiny brown knapsack along with his dragging rope and extra shells. He put on his red-and-black-checkered woolen hunting clothes, the fit like a long-worn glove, shouldered his knapsack and picked up his Winchester bolt action rifle, gently caressing the smoothness of the tightly figured fiddleback hard maple, the balance and heft of a relic that had once

been his father's, a custom-built instrument of precision for use only by men who appreciated the crafts-
manship involved, a smooth-working instrument of
death.

He stared into the darkness of the cabin. Unbelievable, so of course the others refused to believe. He
rubbed at the stubble on his face, the beginning of
his annual beard. Quietly he opened the front door
and slipped out into the penetrating chill of a northwoods winter at six o'clock in the morning. He
stepped lightly away and the shack was almost immediately lost in the vastness of the forest. The stars
were still out, brilliant. Through the naked limbs of
the poplars the morning star shone brightly against
the pale rise of a freezing dawn. Low on the horizon
opposite from the dawn, a three-quarter moon reflect-
ed its blue light off the snow. Something fluttered in
the tree tops and a large white snow owl whooshed
away into the night. Minutes later a noiseless shadow
slipped through the trees off to one side, a tiny black
weasel that had taken refuge.

Eventually he stirred and moved deeper into the
forest, concentrating on moving and seeing without
being seen, working himself into complete alertness,
acute feeling, a mountain man pitting himself against
the wildest elements. He tasted the cold, fresh air,
smelled the tang of a nearby pine, heard the rustle of
the first early morning breeze, saw the emerging
shapes of trees and brush standing upright in the covering snow. He stood as if naked, sensing when the
temperature rose or fell, when the barometer
dropped. Enough.

Less than a half hour of his journey into the forest
he turned, circling wide of his tracks, back to the hill
behind the shack. There he settled in, concealed by a
small clump of balsams, the shack and the two jeeps
clearly visible. He waited.

For almost two hours after Norm had slipped quietly into the forest, nothing moved in the shack. Snoring, grunts and creaking mattresses resounded in the back bunkrooms. The liquor and smoke and grease smells hung motionless beneath the canopy of antlers in the rafters.

Eventually, like black bears emerging from the throes of hibernation, they began to stir, to groan, to bring themselves back into life. Glenn rose first, walking stiff-legged, feeling his way to the bathroom where he threw down four aspirin and tried to focus on the face in the mirror. He'd had a couple too many. Barbara was right to ban liquor from the house. Absolutely right.

Half the night he'd lain there, waiting on Norm. Hour after hour—then suddenly he had awakened and it was daylight. But where had Norm gone? And to do what, he wondered as he carefully washed and shaved and flossed his teeth.

One by one the others, bleary-eyed, stiff and filled with pain, shuffled into the main room and gradually roused themselves for a day already two hours gone. "Got a big head again, don't ya, doc?" Butch called, trying to sound cheerful. Glen could only nod, shuffling silently around with the others. They drifted about, readying their gear: Merald wiping down his three expensive deer rifles, making his daily selection; Bernie muttering as he grudgingly prepared the breakfast of runny eggs and scorched bacon; Rod sitting at the kitchen table, his back to the others, looking out the window at his fourteen-pointer and telling them how he was going to have the head mounted; Butch pacing impatiently with a cup of coffee, waiting for breakfast; David sitting on a couch in the living room, watching them all.

"Hey, what the fuck's going on here?" Butch finally spoke up. "Balls, everyone walks around here like a goddamn zombie. What the hell gives?"

"I don't know," Merald said. The real estate developer sat on the sofa in a tent of white thermal underwear, all three rifles still laid out before him. He chewed on the stub of an unlit cigar. "Something seems different, that's for sure. Maybe it's Norm." He looked to the others for confirmation.

Butch put his coffee cup down. "Why is it everything always is about Norm?"

"That's the way it is," Rod said. "Norm doesn't say much, but he's a doer. I admit that. The only way with Norm is to outdo him, like I did with that fourteen-pointer. That stuck in his craw bad. You could see that clear."

"What do you think about this deal with Norm?" Merald asked, spitting a piece of tobacco on the floor.

"I don't know," Butch said. "There was a time I'd never question Norm. But you know how he's been lately. Look at that deal at the television factory. Something's going on. Maybe things are getting to him. You've heard about his old lady. Maybe he found out."

"That was inevitable," Rod said. "Joannie's a good-looking piece for a guy like Norm."

"The deal at the factory is part of it," Merald said. "I've never seen anyone throw it away like that. A promotion to production management and he turns it down. Damn, I just think of all the years I sweated and gambled and slaved my ass off. And then to turn your back on all those years. . . ." He shook his head.

"Probably is the pressure," Glenn agreed. "You get your life screwed around like Norm's has been lately and the mind can start doing funny things."

"Look at it this way," Butch said. "If someone took a pop at you, you'd go screaming to the cops so damn fast it'd make your head spin. So would I. So why didn't Norm?"

"Norm's a funny guy," Merald said. "Except with

Joannie he's independent as hell. You know how he likes to do things by himself, take off by himself. Just like he hunts up here. Takes off alone before dawn and comes back after dark. Remember a couple years ago when he cut his foot chopping wood? Never said a word. Walked right past us into the john and wrapped it in a bandage. The only reason we found out was because of his bloody sock in the wastebasket. Stuffed underneath everything. Thirty-two stitches they put in that foot. And he never said a word. The guy's like that. Keeps things to himself."

"Yeah, but we're not talking about a cut foot," Butch said. "He's talking about people shooting people. Maybe he got some weird notion to start doing some shooting himself, and this is his way of warning us. Hell, I don't know."

"Anybody shoots at me and I'll kill the bastard," Rod put in.

Bernie, serving up the eggs, protested in his thick voice, "Norm's a good friend. We all know it. Anytime I needed a buck Norm was there. This is just . . . just, ah, a phase or something." He hacked deep in his throat, his face going almost blue, eyes deep in his skull. He leaned over the wastebasket as he coughed and spit phlegm, his eyes watering with the effort.

"What about the business of swimming under the ice," Merald said, trying to ignore Bernie. "That's the part that got me."

"Look, the main point is that Norm's dreaming this stuff up for a reason," Glenn said. "He needs help, bad."

"Maybe a shrink," Rod said, and smiled. "Either that or some pussy. Maybe Joannie's been holding out on him and he's pussy starved. That'll screw a guy up good."

"This is serious," Glenn said.

"Yeah, goddamnit, Rod," Butch said, "do you always have to mouth off?"

"Ah, get fucked," Rod said.

"Easy," Merald cautioned before Butch started to get up.

"Rod has a point. What Norm needs is a doctor," Glenn went on. "How do we get him to one?"

"Where the hell can you get a psychiatrist up here?" Merald asked.

"I don't know," Glenn said softly. "It's either get one up here or wait until we get back to Chicago. Maybe Joannie could talk him into going in."

"Piss on it," Butch said. "I don't want to get all that involved in another man's life. I think Norm'll come around. Basically I think he's pretty solid. Besides, the one thing that convinces me he's just telling stories is the way he brought this up, then let it drop. I don't think he's really that worried."

"Yeah, that's for sure," Merald had his gun picked out. "It was almost like an afterthought. I say forget it."

"Let's get the fuck out of here and do some hunting," Butch said, getting up. "Norm's already out. That's hardly like a guy who's really worried about snipers in the woods. If he gets too wild we'll tie the fucker down and haul him in to the nearest shrink for a reaming out."

"I think Norm's beyond help anyhow," Rod grinned.

Butch ignored Rod. "Let's take a drive. We could head up toward those slashings, maybe drive some of those forties up there. I don't feel like standing around here in the goddamn woods by myself. Nothing much moves the second day, anyhow, unless someone kicks it up."

"Sounds good," Merald said.

"I might hang around here," Glenn said. "Take a little walk later on."

"Suit yourself," Butch said. "But since you already have your buck, I thought maybe you could help the rest of us out by driving. That's the way we've worked in the past."

"Ah, well, sure." Glenn went along, knowing the rules.

Slowly, taking their time, they began to suit up for the day's hunt, long underwear, wool socks, wool pants, flannel shirts and thick coats and mittens. In an hour they left the cabin, rifles encased for the drive.

Norm was just coming out of the woods, working his way down the slight hill at one side of the shack. "Going for a ride?" he asked.

"Yeah," Butch said. "Might make some drives up in the slashings. You coming?"

"Sure, why not?" Norm said, aware they were all watching him, waiting for him to say something. "I'll just get my gun case," he said and headed for the shack.

"You see anything?" Bernie asked.

"A couple of flags," Norm said over his shoulder.

"At least you were out there," Bernie called as Norm went into the shack. "We should have set an alarm like yesterday," he said to the others.

"Well, set one then," Merald said through puffs of smoke from a fat cigar. "You can get up. *I* like to relax now and then. I don't come up here to bust my ass."

"Let's go," Butch said when Norm came back and shut the door. They piled into the two four-wheel-drive jeeps and set out.

Like many other hunters on this second day of the season, they drove slowly, cruising the back roads, peering intently into the forest for their quarry, rifles at their sides, bullets in hand, CB radios squawking, the heater throwing a steady stream of warm air.

They worked the two enclosed jeeps together, driving the roads covering both sides of the woods, using the radios to talk back and forth.

Once, in early afternoon, they stopped and everyone except Norm got out to decide what to do next, each of them suggesting different areas, debating how to set up a deer drive, who would stand and who would make the walk through the forest driving the deer toward the standers, how to arrange the jeeps and riders. For fifteen minutes they argued back and forth while the first heavy flakes of a coming snowfall fell around them. Eventually Bernie stuck his head back inside Rod's jeep and asked Norm what he thought about making a drive down across from the old dynamite shack.

"Sounds okay to me."

Just before they reached the area they had decided to drive, two deer trotted across the road in front of Butch's lead jeep. Merald jammed on the brakes and the jeep slid sideways on the snow-covered dirt road. Butch, riding shotgun, half jumped, half fell out the right-hand door while the jeep was still moving. Agile for his size, he darted around the front of the jeep, ripped off his gun case, jammed home a clip and chambered a shell into his auto-loader. There were five loud reports in quick succession and he had emptied his rifle into the forest in the direction the deer had fled. "Nice buck," he shouted as Rod pulled the second jeep up alongside. "Looked about like a six-pointer. Let's spread out in here and get after it. You guys drop off along the road up around the corner and work back this way. Maybe we can push him in between. Let's go, let's go." He waved them past.

"We're on our way," Rod called back and raced the jeep ahead, sideslipping it around the corner, edging in alongside a snowbank and gunning it to shoot back into the road again. "Gotta go," he said to the men inside, laughing, and flooring the accelerator, and fishtailing the back end wildly. A few hundred feet down the road he jammed on the brakes and slid sideways to a stop. "You get off here, Glenn," he yelled, then sped on, dropping off Bernie and, a couple of hundred yards further, Norm. A quarter mile up the hill beyond Norm's position Rod parked the jeep and cut into the woods himself, all of them heading back toward the area where Butch and his group were spreading out.

Norm slid three shells into his rifle and stepped through the snowbank into the foot-deep snow in the woods. He shook his head. Spread out and run. From a hunting point of view it made little sense. They'd all be moving and odds were the deer would spot them first. It was strictly hit or miss, disorganized, but at least it got him out of the smoky confines of the jeep and into the forest.

He moved slowly, a dark shadow, the sound of his passing muffled by the whisper of heavy snowflakes dropping steadily now between the naked limbs of the poplars, large families of smaller flakes clinging together for their soft flight to the earth, the clusters of white touching and melting on the roughened face, tiny beads of wetness that ran into his mouth.

Several times he heard shots, a flurry from an automatic, and later a couple of single shots from different rifles. But the falling snow soaked up the sounds so he couldn't be certain of the direction or distance. He moved on, once catching the shadow of possibly running deer jumped by one of the others. But he did not pause or raise his rifle.

Somehow the day before seemed to have happened in the distant past. Now he was here and he kept up a sharp vigilance, moving slowly, avoiding open areas, watching all around. He carried his Winchester bolt-action rifle cross arms, the hard maple smooth in his large hands. Without needing to think about it, he moved with great precision, as much a part of the forest as he'd ever been, once again, for the first time in years, fully and joyously involved in the hunt.

CHAPTER VIII

Once out of sight of the others, Glenn had turned his
reversible hunting hat inside out, converting it from
blaze orange to green and brown camouflage ma-
terial. He carried his rifle with both hands, aware
of its feel. He took off one mitten and ran the palm
of his right hand over the smooth finish on the stock,
caressed the cold barrel and stared at the brass point
of a bullet. He held the rifle close to his chest,
touching his cheek to the cold metal, swinging the
scope to center on Barbara's thin, detached face, and
then on the eyes behind Glenn Sr.'s thick glasses,
seeing the puzzlement, the first signs of fear. He lowered the rifle and quietly laughed, the stirring deep
in his loins, a surge pushed by an awareness that he
had grown, become taller, more powerful than before. And they knew it. . . .

He raised his rifle and peered through the scope,
lining the crosshairs up on a tree, his finger touching
at the curve of the trigger, taking up the slack. Just a
little more pressure, he knew, and he could blow
away whatever he wanted. Whatever he wanted. "So
simple. So damn simple."

He laughed again to the sky and as quickly cursed

at the falling snow. With these thick clusters of flakes
and low, dark clouds, the restricted visibility isolated
him from the others. In the back of his head he knew
he was working his way north with the intent of cutting someone's track and finding a figure in black-
and-red-checked hunting clothes. So despite the cover
the storm offered, he cursed its persistent darkness.

Be patient, wait, he told himself and pressed on.
Just to look, he thought, to see what Norm was up
to. . . . He moved cautiously, hunched over,
muscles knotted as he dropped to one knee every few
paces and peered beneath the low branches around
him, excitement steadily increasing with the
knowledge that Norm might actually be looking to
find *him*.

"And then?" Norm was supposed to be predictable,
but the way he'd behaved in the shack last night—?
Why didn't Norm accuse him, go to the police? Why
did he allow their ridicule. . . , What was he
waiting for? Unless he hadn't seen him, or wasn't certain . . . but he must have seen him. . . . Had
he decided, foolhardy, to reverse the roles of hunter
and hunted . . . ?

He bent low to the deep snow, squinting to pick up
the sight of moving legs. He had to consciously control his breathing, the night before was still very
much with him—Norm coming through the forest
helping to drag Rod's buck, the terror, how close he'd
come to folding up and falling to the ground . . .
and Norm never said a word. . . .

He shook his head once, summoning his self-control. Outwardly he'd given them nothing. Swam under the ice, Norm had said, and everyone had hooted.
Insanity, he'd suggested, and the others had picked it
up. A quiet laugh escaped him, the way the others
jumped on Norm about his frozen clothes, his far-
fetched story . . . even *seeing*, they would not believe. He tried to imagine their shock, their disbelief,

if they knew. Insanity—his best tack, his key. Just keep it going. . . .

He remembered Norm sitting at the card table, so damn quiet, calm, not even the courtesy to show some emotion. Glenn sucked rhythmically at the cool, clean air, but still felt his muscles going taut . . . I'm here, the big man had said, I swam under the ice to survive. Under the ice. And now I'm waiting. . . .

The man truly was insane, Glenn thought, shaking his head and wrapping his arms around the pain in his belly—an ulcer, he worried. When the pain subsided he dusted the snow from his rifle with a dry handkerchief, wiping the scope carefully and checking to see that the lens wasn't fogged before replacing the lens cover. He lowered his head, eyes clenched tight. If only he hadn't done the first one.

But he had.

After a time he picked himself up and began to move, pausing often to reconnoiter his flanks and front. The scenes of trees and blurred brush and falling snow repeated themselves every few paces, the picture unchanged no matter how far he moved. So old Norm knew . . . and was waiting for him? Was that it? His stomach clutched once again.

And again he sighted through the scope, his mind's eye placing a red-and-black-checked hunting coat on a distant tree, bringing the crosshairs to bear with trembling hands, the movement growing so violent he lost sight of his target. He rubbed his eyes with the back of his mitten, aware of the deep pain in his breast, of the bile coursing through his body to provide a sour taste in his mouth.

Fifteen minutes later, far away down a gentle slope to his left, he glimpsed red. He froze in a crouch but lost sight of it in the thick falling snow, the darkness of the storm, and the heavy trees and brush of the white forest. He stepped sideways, moving his head back and forth in order to see through tiny crevices in the forest. *There*—a man, all right, dressed in the red-and-black-checked clothing he'd been looking for.

The world stopped. He hesitated, drawing back. But the time for *that* had long since passed. Resigned, he stepped forward, moving to one side of the slight opening in the trees, occasionally pausing to check that the man could be seen. He moved as he thought a ballet dancer must on stage—on tiptoe, with finely controlled tension flooding every part of his body, step by careful step, a snowman covered with rime, his breath billowing. What had so worried him, he admitted, was knowing how well Norm could hunt, how well he moved about in the forest. But by god there Norm was, down the hill, looking the other way this time, still as if a statue mounted on a pedestal, oblivious. . . .

He slid in behind a large poplar. Close enough. He peeked out from behind the tree and saw old Norm still standing patiently down the hill. His blood began to race.

"He's waiting for us," he said in a slow voice of discovery. His skin prickled with the knowledge of how they felt, of what they wanted him to do. "Be careful. Protect yourself," they always said. He was grateful for them, their support. . . .

Carefully he eased his rifle around the tree, left arm braced against the trunk for support, right arm reaching to remove the scope cover. The darkness all but concealed the thin crosshairs of his scope, but there he stood, a dark outline, big, tall Norm Petrie. He released the safety catch. Shouldn't have waited, Norm. Shouldn't have waited.

The curve of the cold metal trigger touched his forefinger, a union of the power of the rifle, a cocked firing pin, a silently waiting bullet. All he had to do was gently squeeze one finger. The absurdity. His body surged, a dizziness in his mind. "Be calm, be calm," he cautioned, recalling the girl hunter standing silently in the forest, oblivious like Norm, and how then she was crawling, a useless, senseless crawl for thirty feet through snow only to be stopped by a six-inch log.

Only Norm should be the one to take care, but he didn't act, just stood there. Glenn grinned, teeth barely showing, his finger toying with the trigger, the crosshairs centered on the red and black. He shivered. And pulled the trigger.

The image jumped, snow flew, darkness clouded his senses. He leaned forward, searching frantically down the hill, the stab in his guts commanding that he turn and escape before Norm began to move. But there, yes there. A body lying sideways in the snow. Definitely a body.

What now when they found the body?

Abruptly, as if pulled by a gigantic hand, he whirled and made for the road, taking a path wide of his victim, rushing so he would be there with the others.

By the time he stumbled out onto the snow-covered road he was breathing heavily and covered with sweat. Two hundred yards up the road he spotted the jeep. Most of the others were spread out along the road or straggling out of the forest, the exhaustion of the hunt clear in their dogged movements.

They gathered at the front of the jeep and popped cans of beer, leg muscles quivering from the exertion of their hunt, muttering and cursing the lack of success and the weather and the fact that Norm was still back in the forest.

Glenn turned away to conceal his delight at their irritation with Norm. Norm had always bothered them—his dreaming, his high ideals, and now his stories. The man didn't fit. But the minute they learned he was dead . . . he shook his head. It'd be good ol' Norm then.

"There he is," someone said.

Panic, like a roundhouse sledgehammer blow into Glenn's guts. His knees all but buckled. There, climbing down through the snow bank, a figure was moving in slow motion, a tall figure in black-and-red hunting clothes—Norm.

CHAPTER IX

There's a dead hunter up in the woods," Norm an-
nounced as he approached, looking them straight in
the face. "He was shot in the back sometime in the
last half hour."

"You gotta be kidding," Bernie said.

"Are you sure?" Rod asked.

"I'll be a sonofabitch," Butch said.

"How far back?" Merald asked.

"About a half mile," Norm said through his teeth.
To a man they appeared genuinely surprised,
shocked, gathering around him like vultures around a
freshly dead carcass. Was he absolutely positive the
man was dead? Who was the guy? How old? Did he
see anyone else, or any tracks? Where was the guy
shot? Hadn't he thought to check the man's wallet?
Question after question, from every one of them, so
fast that Norm didn't have time to observe their re-
sponses carefully. He tried to keep an eye on Rod
and Butch, at least.

Glenn coughed to clear his throat. "We better in-
form the authorities before it gets dark," he said,
looking at the others for affirmation. None of them
seemed particularly keen to go see what a rifle bullet

would do to a man's body. They just stared, slack-jawed, dwarfed under the sheer cliff of a huge mountain.

"Who should we contact?" Glenn asked in a tight voice.

"Contact?" Merald asked, almost laughing to cover his anxiety.

"Yeah," Glenn said, his voice hushed by the thickly falling snow that continued to gather on their heads and shoulders and on the black jeep a few feet away. The freshly opened beer cans were forgotten in their hands. "It's our legal obligation to report an accident like this. Otherwise the authorities could arrest us for failing to report an accident, and also for leaving the area."

"I was shooting in there," Merald blurted. "And— and so was Butch. I didn't see anyone, though. I didn't." He looked from one man to another, searching for confirmation.

"That's right," Butch said. "We both shot in here. What if one of our bullets accidentally hit this guy?"

Merald moaned, sinking as if his knees were weak. "Think of the publicity. It'd ruin me."

"What about me?" Rod asked. "I've got more to lose than you."

"I shot in there too, but an accident still has to be reported," Glenn said, his normally calm tone taking on an exasperated edge. "What's wrong with you guys? If there's no outright negligence, they'll drop the matter. They won't bother about a stray bullet. But they'll nail you good if you don't report it."

"What about the other two dead hunters?" Norm said.

"What the fuck does that have to do with it?" Rod spoke up indignantly, playing the ex-marine strutting in front of the employees of his father-in-law's mobile home manufacturing plant, letting them know *he* was now in charge of production—and that they would produce or—

Norm avoided the trap. "I'm not saying anything," he answered slowly, "except that this is the third hunter killed in these two counties in the last four years."

"What are we going to do?" Merald asked, his voice shaky. Like the time of his auto accident on the freeway during rush hour. Sixty miles an hour, bumper to bumper and the world came apart—metal, dust, a car looming, his hands leaving the wheel strangely, the car slewed sideways, then punched in the rear corner by a skidding semi truck and catapulted across two lanes of traffic onto the median. Unhurt, Merald had claimed he could not even stand, his back and neck—which had earned him twenty thousand dollars from the insurance company and his start in real estate.

"We don't have any choice," Glenn said. "We have to get the law. Show them the body. Tell them what we know."

"Dammit to hell, there goes the season," Butch muttered, shifting his muscled bulk back and forth. "They'll be at us, questioning us for days."

"What if they ask about the other hunters that were shot?" Bernie asked, his gaunt face ashen. "Like that girl that was shot last year. We were down that way."

"We talked about that last year, Bernie," Rod grumbled. "We don't know anything about that. That's a big area. We didn't even hear about it until several days afterward."

"Yeah, but we *were* down there," Bernie said quickly. "We were."

"Maybe they will ask about it," Merald said. "If they find out we hunted down where that girl was, they'll have us on the grill for two weeks. They might even try to frame us just so they can say they got an arrest."

"That happened on Kojak one night," Bernie said, his voice tight with excitement.

"Shut the fuck up, Bernie," Butch said. "Don't you understand what the fuck this means? Say Merald or I hit this guy in here with a stray shot. I fired that clip from the road and one more at a couple of flags. Say the cops trace that to my gun, or Merald's gun. They'll jump to conclusions so fast it won't be funny. And just because of an accident."

"It's still best to report it," Glenn said, holding his hand out as if to caution the others, pleased with how well it was going . . . once he'd gotten over the shock of it not being Norm, of having been *mistaken*. . . .

"Ah, shit." Butch looked disgusted. "I suppose we better." He made the decision for all of them. He guzzled the rest of his beer and absentmindedly crushed the can in one hand. He squinted at the others, a drill sergeant about to chew out a platoon of raw recruits. He spat a stream of tobacco at their feet. "But not one goddamn word about us hunting down where that girl was killed. We drive down that way, fine. But no one recalls for certain if we were in there last year. Let's get 'em off our backs as soon as possible. A couple of us will stay here and the rest can go report this."

"That sounds pretty good." Merald wiped at the sweat on his face.

Norm thought about these men gathered in a small huddle in front of the jeep, rifles and beers in hand, shoulders hunched against the cold and falling snow. He had just told them a man had died and now they were angered that the pattern of *their* lives had been so rudely upset. Even now, after he'd reminded them about the other deaths in past years, and had told them earlier about being shot at himself, the meaning

of it hadn't sunk in, could not enter when their
minds—all but one—had not been prepared. Were
closed.

Nothing in Norm's expression revealed what he
knew they—all but one—were not willing to consider
. . . that within this group the killer looked him in
the face. He spoke carefully. "We don't have to report this, you know." They were all ears. "If we do
report it, the police won't let us be. They'll eventually tie this in with the other two, the girl and that
man two years ago. As far as I know, we're the only
lead they've got. They can't afford to let us be."

"What do you mean, lead?" Butch demanded. "An
accident happened. So what the fuck? What the hell
are you saying?"

"I'm simply saying that maybe this is something we
could handle ourselves. I've always thought it's best
to face problems head-on, by oneself."

"What?" Merald couldn't believe this.

"You're crazy, Norm," Glenn said, bending forward
to peer into Norm's face. "How can you think like
that? A man has just been killed. You found him.
You *did,* didn't you?"

"No, no. I get it," Butch said, holding up a hand
for silence. He stared at Norm, struggling to hold
back a grin. "I think old Norman here has suckered
us again. The thought crossed my mind when he first
spoke up, but I got sucked in just like everyone else. I
should have known. It's just like yesterday when
someone supposedly shot at him and he swam under
the ice to save his life. And then this morning he gets
up and goes hunting. Getting shot at, a swim under
the ice? All forgotten? There was no one after him
yesterday. No more than there's a dead body up in
those woods. It's just more of Norm's bullshit."

"Maybe you better go see a doctor, Norm." Glenn
had finally said it. It was the right time. Poor Norm.

"Sure as hell," Rod said. "It's all made up. Norm's just fucked in the head."

"And we believed it," Butch said.

"What're you doing, Norm?" Bernie asked, his tone pained. "I don't know what's going on anymore." His voice trailed off.

Merald smiled, laughing with Butch. He wrapped his arm around David's shoulders, pulling the fat little boy to his side. "I used to think you were pretty dependable, Norm. You always took the lead in getting things organized out here. I don't know what, but something's changed, something's gone haywire."

"It's that fourteen-pointer I got," Rod said. "Norm's feeling the pressure."

"The truth now," Glenn said, almost allowing his voice to rise. "Norm, did you find a body up there?"

"Yes. There's a body up there, about a half mile back."

"Don't let him buffalo you, doc," Butch said. "As long as he's got one fish on the line he'll keep it up."

"So let's go take a look," Glenn said. "If there's anything at all to this we definitely should know."

"I ain't walking back up in that woods in this snow," Merald said. "I'm with Butch. Norm's stringing us along again. Just like yesterday."

"I think we've got to look," Glenn said.

"And then what?" Rod asked. "It's less than an hour until dark. We should play Norm's game and go stumble around following him on a wild goose chase through the woods? He'd probably get us lost. No, you go, doc. Tonight's Hurley night. I'm going back to the shack and clean up. I've got a rack of horns a yard long. And some young dolly's going to help me get dehorned right pronto."

"That's what I say," Merald put in.

"Tell me the truth." Glenn allowed himself to stare up into Norm's face. "Is there a body up there? Should we go look?"

"There's a body up there," Norm said, "but it doesn't matter if we look or not."

"*Listen* to that bullshit," Butch howled. "Who'd believe it?"

"Not even a shrink," Rod said.

(Or the police, Norm feared, which was why he had finally advised against going to them.)

"There's nothing up there but more snow." Butch tossed his empty beer can over the snowbank and started toward the jeep. "Come on, I'm up for a little pussy tonight. Let's get the fuck out of here before we get attacked by monsters."

The others laughed, then they all loaded into the jeeps and headed for the shack, those riding with Norm staring ahead or out the windows at the passing forest and falling snow. The light of day was all but gone. A half mile up the road they passed a small group of hunters standing beside the road, apparently waiting for the last of their group to leave the forest. No one waved. And all the way to the shack no one spoke.

CHAPTER X

Glenn stood in the shack bathroom, the cold water turned on full blast as he bent over the sink, sloshing handfuls of icy water into his face.

He'd been positive it was Norm. Red and black hunting outfit. He hadn't quite seen the face, true, but the sight was good. The shot good. It *should* have been him.

The injustice. Of course at first he'd never had any intentions with Norm. At first, just looking. But this. He'd shot Norm in the creek and Norm had come back. And now he shot Norm in the midst of the falling snow and Norm had come back, claiming there was a dead hunter up there. The snow was magic, charmed. . . .

You big rotten sonofabitch, he wanted to scream at the top of his lungs, his loaded rifle in hand, the stock smooth to his grip, the metal and wood jumping as he jerked at the trigger again and again. Wham. Wham. Wham. Tiny pieces of lead slamming Norm up against the refrigerator, holding him there while blood came from his chest, his sad brown eyes big and wide with surprise.

Here? In front of the others?

Yes, Norm, here.

In a few minutes Glenn wound down and stared into the mirror at his dripping face. No quivering there now. The face a little tanned, clean, wet sandy hair balding at the front, appeared quiet, thoughtful. "You even *look* like a dentist," Glenn Sr. had said that graduation day, his arms around Glenn Jr.'s shoulders.

The thought of Glenn Sr. banked the fire. "I didn't do anything wrong, dad," Glenn explained in a whisper to his image in the mirror. "Norm's lying. There's no body. Norm's just baiting, making up stories. You heard the others." He nodded. "I know he is."

When Glenn returned to the living room Norm was outside fetching an armful of wood and the others were talking about him.

"We've got to get Norm to a doctor," Butch was saying. "I think the man's in a bad way."

"He might take a notion to pull his knife to protect himself," Rod said, rolling his eyes. "All these killers he sees."

"Rod, this is serious. Norm needs help and we have to do something."

"Yeah, Rod," Merald said, siding with Butch.

"Well, do something then," Rod said. "Go tell him, Merald." His voice got deep, authoritative. "Norm, we think you're crazy. We're taking you to a shrink. C'm'on along, boy." He looked at Merald, challenging him. Merald didn't rise to it.

"That's going to be a problem," Glenn said quietly. "Convincing Norm isn't going to be easy. And I doubt there's a psychiatrist within fifty miles. We might have to try to hold on until we get back to Chicago."

"You think we can afford to wait?" Butch asked.

Glenn shrugged, and as he did Norm pushed into the kitchen with an armful of firewood. He noted their silence, then crossed to dump the logs in the woodbox beside the fireplace. He straightened, staring, a deep silence between them and him.

After supper everyone except young David was to make the annual drive into Hurley. "Come on," Butch said to the protests of not feeling up to the drive. "We go every year. So we go this year. Nothing's changed. Got that, Norm?" he said, pointing his finger in Norm's face.

Norm stared back, unblinking, a man taking in the scenery. "Sure. Why not? Let's go into town. Celebrate Rod's record buck. We'll have a ball."

Butch glanced sideways at Norm. "C'm'on fella . . . take it easy . . . put on your duds and let's get going. The pussy is just snapping, waiting on us to get there. Just what the doctor ordered."

"Yeeeeha," Rod said, and jumped to his feet. "First round's on me. Got to celebrate the shack's record buck, for sure."

Quickly they changed and departed for Hurley, a small town thirty miles away on the Michigan-Wisconsin border that had once been famous for its gambling and prostitution. The atmosphere and vestiges of the old gambling, logging and prohibition days remained as each year thousands of red-coated hunters crowded into the town to throw down their two dollars for a bottle of beer.

First stop was the Silver Slipper, an ancient, dark bar with the lights turned so low they could barely recognize each other. The stately back bar towered over the proceedings, a carved oak border with an arched cathedral mirror in the center and stacked bottles of liquor lining the entire front. Even though it was Sunday night, hunters and six or eight women lined the bar. At one side a middle-aged woman wearing high heels, pasties and a spangled string bikini, the folds of her flesh dimpled and sagging, moved listlessly around on a small stage.

"Eeeeehaaa," Butch yelped to announce their arrival, and they ventured forward into the murky darkness of the tavern with the babble of voices and jukebox and neon lights and unseen faces. The men began to curse and laugh and strut. And the women, the tired wrinkles of their thickly painted faces unseen in the dark, cracked smiles and gathered around.

"Well if it isn't the boys from Trail's End," Big Renetta said with a laugh, moving into the midst of their small circle. She was a large woman, appearing to be in her mid-thirties in the dark, crowding fifty according to some of those who'd seen her in daylight. She wore a black mini-dress that showed off large thighs covered by black net stockings. She laughed a good one as Butch seized her in a bear hug. "Damn you, Butch. You're going to break my back."

"Hey, Renetta," he said, and touched at the side of her right breast. "Looks like there's a tad bit more there this year."

"Well, it looks like there's more than a tad bit there," she countered, poking at Butch's protruding stomach.

"Fit as a fiddle," Butch said, smacking his gut. "Have a drink."

"Sure thing, Butch. Make it a brandy. The boss knows my flavor. . . . And how are ya doing there, Rodney?" Renetta asked, peering into the dark. "Still the handsome ladies' man, huh? You up for three on one night?" She was referring to the time four years ago when Rod had been up and down the back stairs with three different women. "Three in one night," he'd boasted for the rest of the season. "How many of you guys ever done that?"

"No, not tonight," Rod told her. "But I would like to get to know that silver mink over there." He nodded toward a tall platinum blonde woman out on the dance floor in tight black silk pants, a black silk blouse unbuttoned down the front and red high-heeled shoes. "Look at those moves," he said. "I think I wanna hold her gland." He ran a comb through his curly blond hair. "I think I'm in love."

"Yeah, and the only way you've ever spelled love is F.U.C.K." Renetta said, and everyone laughed.

"As good a way as any," Rod said, "probably better than most. . . . Hey, Renetta, I shot a fourteen-point buck yesterday. Wiped out all of old Norm's shack records once and for all."

"Do we have to hear that again," Merald moaned.

"I'm surprised he waited so long to bring it up," Butch said.

"Well, congratulations, Rodney," Renetta said. "That must have broke poor Norm's heart. He hasn't said a word all night." She looked at Norm, who met her eyes and gave her a friendly nod. "You should celebrate," she said to Rod. "The blonde is Cherry. No shit. Ask her to dance."

"I'll just do that," Rod said, and strode across the dance floor. "Hi, Cherry, the name is Rod." He broke up.

The woman shrugged.

Butch pulled Renetta out onto the dance floor and wrapped his large arms around her, pressing the bulk of her flesh close to his, laughing, working against her laughing protests through the silk of her dress to unhook her bra. "An eight-hooker," he roared after-ward. "An eight-hooker. Now if that isn't a record, I don't what what is."

While Butch and Renetta danced and Rod went off with Cherry, two other women, motioned over by Renetta, approached the others. One of them, a tall, rounded Italian girl with coal-black hair and olive skin, moved in next to Merald. She forced a smile. "Hi. Out on the town for a little fun?"

"Huh? Oh, yeah, out for a few drinks." He slid his bulk sideways, one leg off the bar stool, braced on the floor. He glanced at the woman's dark eyes, then quickly away, downed his drink and slid it across for a refill. "Want a drink?"

"Sure. You from Chicago?"

"Yeah. I'm in real estate," Merald said, his face sweating, "apartment buildings, housing developments, a little land speculation. You know."

"Yeah, I know," she said and ordered the drink. She moved closer to Merald, her hand sliding up his thigh, feeling the big man tremble.

Next to her a tall bony redhead had crowded in beside Glenn, her not-so-young body tight against his side, her arm around his shoulders. "How about it, Mr. Dentist," she was saying, "let's take a little walk. Beats the old drill."

"No, thanks," Glenn mumbled softly, his eyes fixed on the bar.

"Why not?" Her face, even through the makeup, appeared parched, her eyes blue and thickly outlined with mascara. She tried to smile at the balding man beside her; the effort went unnoticed.

Glenn shook his head without turning. She was at least ten years his senior, trying to talk him into a walk upstairs. The thought of her wrinkled body churned into his stomach. He glanced at her sideways, as if to say something, and couldn't avoid her sunken, tired eyes. "Come on, Red," he said quietly. "What say I buy you a drink anyhow."

"No walk?"

"No. No, I think not." His mind was on Barbara now, on the way she lay there making her little circles on his back. Something women had to put up with, her mother had said time and again. And her body still believed.

Glenn glanced about, the darkness of the bar homing in, the familiarity painful like the memory of his own living room. Fifteen years they'd been coming here. And the taverns never changed. Each time some unseeing girl would be bouncing her flesh on the stage while a crowd of sweaty hunters would be waddling around in their dirty outfits, spilling drinks, grabbing at the women who worked the bar. And, except for the pale blue spotlight on the stage, they were always wrapped in darkness, faces hidden, the jukebox blasting out tinny music to fill up the void.

"Insanity," Glenn muttered.

"What's that?" the redhead asked.

"Nothing. People." He turned and made his way down a dark, narrow corridor into the unheated cement bathroom and stepped up to the single urinal. Abruptly the door opened and someone crowded into the tiny room behind him, waiting for him to finish. Glenn paused, his scrotum pulled tight.

He glanced over his shoulder. Norm! A sharp pain sliced up the inside of his spine. Everything in the room became distinct, clearly recognized, to be forever remembered—the room cold with gray cement walls, grimy red cement floor, the dampness of the mortar soaking up the warmth from his skin. The stench of urine was going to overpower him. His mouth filled with a sour phlegm and he leaned back and spat into the urinal.

"What do you think of all these goings-on?" Norm asked, his tone even, firm.

The cheeks of Glenn's ass drew together. "Ah, well, I don't know what to say, Norm."

"Do *you* believe me?"

Glenn shrugged, pulling up his zipper, his left hand feeling for the Luger beneath his shirt, trying to keep turned so he could note any sudden moves. "I don't really know what to believe, Norm. It kind of boggles the mind, as they say." He squeezed past, chest to chest. He glanced up into Norm's face, a massive face, not ugly, strangely intriguing, like a craggy mountain, impassive yet powerful, in perspective from a distance but looming so high up close. The brown eyes were flat, gleaming with light, calm, confident. He knows, Glenn thought. He must . . . he could kill me here.

But in the cool of the corridor outside he wondered otherwise. Maybe he didn't know . . . maybe . . . and if he did, this was the Norm who wouldn't shoot deer anymore. "He's getting old, soft," Glenn argued into the hubbub of the tavern. "He'll lose his nerve . . . just like—"

He cut himself short and continued on into the bar, talking to himself, mumbling, moving up to where Bernie had crowded in behind the redhead, the little slope-shouldered man stumbling and spilling his drink and pushing the woman into the bar. "Oops, sorry," Bernie said. Then, "Listen, lady," tugging at her elbow the way a little boy tugs at his mother's skirt, "you want to take a walk? I'll take a walk. Come on." The redhead ignored him.

"Why ya fucking whore—" Anger from a man who hadn't cared enough to feel any for a long time.

"Hey," Glenn said quietly, and gently grabbed Bernie by the shoulders. "We don't want any trouble here, Bern."

Bernie jerked free as the redhead made her way down the bar. "Bitch," he said in his hoarse voice. "They're all bitches, damn them."

"Have a drink, Bernie," Glenn said and gestured at the bartender to bring another round. He threw a ten on the bar, waiting, glancing back toward the bathroom, wondering what was keeping Norm.

After a few minutes Butch came walking up, holding a piece of paper. "Look at this," he said. "One of the broads gave it to me. It's from Norm, says he's taking my spare key I have taped under the hood and is heading back to the shack. Says he doesn't feel good."

"What? Let me see that?" Glenn had to restrain himself not to grab at the note.

"Goddamn Norm pisses me off. The least he could do was ask first."

Merald looked up over the dark-haired woman's shoulder, sliding sideways from where she'd crowded him next to the bar. "I wonder what's *with* Norm these days. He sure the hell is acting different."

"Crazy," Glenn muttered, rereading the note. "He's got to be."

Rod walked up, patting at his belt buckle to see that it was secure. "Well, that's two scores for the day. How's everyone else doing?"

"Ah, goddamn Norm left a note saying he took my jeep. Didn't feel well or some shit," Butch muttered.

"Norm needs a little pussy," Rod said with a laugh. "Could be that's all that's ailing him. Hey, I wonder what people would do if they didn't have sex?"

"Ask him," the dark-haired woman said, and squeezed Merald's shoulder. "If you ever make up your mind, you know where to find me."

"Yeah, ah, sure." Merald waved her and her six dollars worth of his drinks away. He hadn't asked for her name.

"So what do we do about Norm?" Glenn asked. "Now we *have* to do something."

The others shrugged, standing in front of the towering back bar and its mirrored bottles of liquor. A couple of dozen hunters were crowded up to the bar, a few bargirls mixing in with them. The jukebox blared a fast number and the girl on stage tried to bump and grind to it.

"Screw Norm," Butch said. "Let's have a few drinks and have a good time, like we deserve."

"That's right," Merald said, his large face leering at the girl on stage. "We deserve to cut loose a bit."

The others turned to the bar, ordering a fresh round.

"Stupids," Glenn muttered against the dark and

the music. Moving quickly, he made for the dark of the back hallway and the bathroom, searching all around to assure himself that Norm had indeed left. Farther down the hallway was a closed door. Glenn pushed through it.

Two men sitting across from each other at a desk looked up. "What the hell do you want?" one of them said.

"Ah, just looking for a friend."

"Well, you can see he ain't here, so get the hell moving," one dark-haired man with olive-colored skin said. "And knock next time if you know what's good for you."

"Yeah, okay," Glenn mumbled, and backed out, gently closing the door. He stood in the hallway, shaking inside, and pulled the Luger out of his waistband. "Stupids." He stared at the door and flicked the safety off.

But he had no time. He knew exactly why Norm had left. There was a body. There was probably a search on for the missing hunter. Norm wanted to get off by himself so he could meet with the police. All his talk about not going to them had been nothing but a diversion. . . .

He came back down the corridor, stuffing the pistol back inside his shirt and dogtrotting through the noise and smoke of the dark tavern, darting unseen behind the others and out into the cool air of the winter night. He broke into a run, arms pumping, legs lifted high on the icy sidewalk, his course toward where they'd parked Butch's jeep. He pictured Norm with the police, telling his story. His legs pumped harder.

His feet slid away and he crashed on his side, his wind knocked away.

A powerful hand reached down and took hold of his shoulder. "Have a mite too much to drink there, partner?" a voice said.

"No. No, I just slipped," he said, gasping for air,

head lowered to the sidewalk. He stood and looked into the smiling faces of two policemen, a short thin one and a medium hefty one.

"Looks like you were in quite a hurry," the thin cop remarked.

"A buddy of mine was heading back to camp early and I wanted to try and catch up with him." He tried to draw free from the grip.

"Hold it up there, partner," the beefy cop said, his fingers digging into Glenn's arm. "You seem upset over something more than just your buddy taking off to the shack without you. What gives? You got a problem? You in trouble?"

"No. No," Glenn said, thinking of little else but the Luger hidden under his belt. He hesitated, staring past the cops to where Butch's jeep had been parked. "Goddamn Norm," he said aloud.

"What?" the beefy cop asked.

"Ah . . ."—Glenn focused—"it's just that my partner that took off with the jeep . . . he never even asked, just left." He pulled back.

"You better call it a night," the thin cop said. "Seems to me you've had more than your share to drink—"

"Sure, I'll tell the others and we'll head out," Glenn said, backing away a few steps, then turning and walking back toward the tavern. The SS-styled black Luger materialized in his hand . . . turn and fire, whirl around on them, wide stance, left hand grips the right wrist for support, the automatic pistol bucks as shot after shot jolts them back on their heels and they sprawl in the snow and . . . the bitter taste again . . . "A boy as promising as Glenny shouldn't have to go to school with punks," his father had told the school board that day after fat George Knutson had pushed him to the ground during recess. . . . "Just look at those scrapes. Glenny's going to be a doctor some day, someone special. A bully like that Knutson brat, you should send him to reform school where he belongs. . . ."

"Your fucking-A, dad . . ." Glenn said it aloud, spun around, the Luger leveled, but the sidewalk, of course, was empty. . . .

After a while he walked back into the bar where the others were still bellied up, Rod and Bernie so drunk they could barely see out of their faces. He paused near the entrance, getting accustomed to the dark. Norm gone. He bit his knuckles so hard they bled.

"Hey, Glenn. Come on over. I'm buying a round to celebrate my fourteen-pointer," Rod broadcast from the bar.

Glenn nodded, pushed his bloodied hand into his pocket and walked over to join the others.

CHAPTER XI

Norm made his way from the rear of the tavern to the main street, pausing in the chill of the winter night. A few noisy hunters passed, filling up the icy sidewalk and edging him back against the wall of the tavern. He stood and watched them file into the tavern, then breathed in the cool air, a solitary figure. On the black, slushy street an automobile slid past with barely a sound. The line of old brick taverns along the street stood hunched over as if ashamed of their appearance in the dim yellow streetlights. Neon lights flickered. Prohibition days. Mining days. Lumbering days. And now a quiet small town looking to erase the past. But come deer season and the worst of it revived.

He made his way to Butch's jeep, pleased with the upset his disappearance would cause . . . whichever of them it was. He took the key taped under the hood and left town, driving slowly and carefully down the empty country highways, stopping at Swede's, a backwoods bar that they frequented, located ten miles from the shack. After the usual greetings from the baldheaded Swede and a couple of quiet beers, he walked the length of the bar, past the backbar with the stuffed deer head and the mounted muskie and walleye to the old wood-and-glass-enclosed telephone booth.

Here he hesitated. How could he possibly tell Joannie how it felt not to have to deal with contradictory situations, to at least have a clearly defined role, a clearly defined task. Frightening for what it was, but in its way a relief too, even a pleasure. . . . Besides, she would still be all upset about the way, without even consulting her, he'd turned down the prestige of a production management job and a three-thousand-dollar-a-year raise plus profit sharing. "How could you?" she'd asked over and over. And he shouldn't have been surprised.

He forced himself to dial the number.

"Hello," a young girl's voice said cheerfully, as if she expected the call.

"Kim, this is your father."

"Oh," she said, "you want to talk to mother?"

"Ah . . . no, no, in a minute. Ah, how're things going?"

"Oh, fine. I was just waiting for a call. I'll get mother."

Sweet little Kim, a mover like her mother, honor roll, cheerleader, upward and onward, the little girl he used to hold in his arms and make laugh who now had no more use for him.

"Hello." Joannie was finally on the line.

"Hi. I, ah, just called to see how everything is going."

"Well, fine of course. It's only been three days."

Norm flinched at the tone. "I spoke to Kim. How's Jeffrey?"

"Same as he always is, of course. Off by himself, reading his science fiction, hardly ever saying a word, about anything. . . . he's your son. . . . you should know. . . ."

"Yes," he said softly, peering through the smudged

glass of the booth toward the blurry figures down the length of the tavern, fellow escapees from home and city.

"Did you get anything?"

"What . . . ? Oh, no, I saw a few but no shots—"

"It's just as well, it'd go to waste anyway. Remember the last one."

"Yes. . . . David got a spike, Doc an eight-pointer and Rod shot a fourteen-pointer—"

"Well, isn't that nice. Did you know your buddy Rod hit Sue in the face before he left? Something to remember him by. She didn't *say* so but she had a bruise big as a half dollar on her cheek. Nice guys you buddy-buddy with, big deal he-men out in the woods with their damn rifles—"

"Joannie, I don't want to argue," Norm said, surprised, pleased, at the firmness in his voice. "I just felt I wanted to talk to you. You're my wife. There's a very serious problem up here—"

"What do you mean?"

How to say it? . . . I think one of the guys is a killer. . . . Impossible, she'd laugh at him, say he was crazy, why didn't he go to the police . . . ?

"Yes, what's the problem?" Joannie asked impatiently. "Norm, do you *always* have to take so long thinking about what you're going to say?"

"Ah, you know, Joannie . . . how I've always said that when I die I want to be cremated—"

"Norm! What the hell are you talking about?"

"Well, I'm just saying if an accident or anything happens, I want you to make sure to have my ashes spread around up here by the hunting shack. Out over the seven-mile swamp. The guys know. . . ."

"Sonofabitch, Norm! First the job, now this . . . is this what you called me about?"

"Ah, I'm not sure," hearing the foolishness of his words. "I wanted you to know and I . . . I guess I just wanted to talk to you—"

"Oh, then you've been thinking about what I said?" Joannie said, her voice calming some.

"Oh, yes," Norm said, very slowly.

"And?"

"And what?"

"And *what* are you going to do about it?"

Her words were like a gray weight on his mind. "Well, go on, I guess—"

"Go on! I can't go on, Norm. I thought I made that clear. Things have got to change."

"But why? I mean it, Joannie. What do you change for?"

"Change for? To live, Norm. My god! Have you gone off the deep end or something? You're not even making sense anymore. . . ." There was more but he didn't hear it. He was picturing her smooth, naked body that he hadn't touched for over two months, her flat stomach, her firm thighs, her upturned breasts. The beauty of nature's creation—"Norm, when you get back we're really going to have to talk about whether we should stay together or not. I *mean* it, Norm. . . ."

He stood there silently, sweating, his forehead pressed against the glass, his body leaning against the side of the booth, his legs rubbery, barely able to support his weight.

"Norm?"

"Yes."

"Did you hear?"

"Yes."

"Well?"

"Joannie, I love you."

"Oh, for god's sake, Norm!"

"House still standing?" Swede asked when Norm returned to the bar.

"Still standing," Norm said, playing the game he'd

played all his life. "Kids running wild, the wife out on the town while I'm up here in the woods."

"Just like back in the war, huh?" Swede said. He set a fresh bottle of beer in front of Norm. "Want me to sweeten that with a shot? Seems to me I recall you tossing down a few boilermakers in here one day."

Norm stared, then forced a grin. "That was a long time ago, Swede. But I'll tell you what, you throw the dice and we'll see if maybe you can buy me one."

"You're on," Swede said, wiggling his finger at Norm, his brown eyes saying that he knew more of what went on for Norm then he was saying.

Swede was one damn good man, Norm thought. "Make it a Jack Daniel's," he said. "And pour yourself one too. We might as well start out even."

CHAPTER XII

By the time Norm took the turnoff to the shack it was almost eleven. He drove very slowly, squinting and concentrating on guiding the jeep safely between the closing poplars, the half hour drive a blurred passage of time he could not remember.

The others had already returned, he noted with surprise as he pulled up in front of the shack. Apparently they'd arrived only a few minutes before him. The shack's lights were all on. He stopped to urinate in the snow, swaying a little back and forth, once stepping forward to catch his balance. The sound of laughter carried from inside the shack. They had visitors, women. Well, what the hell, he thought. . . .

The door burst open and a shaft of light hit Norm in the face. "Hey, Petrie, what the fuck you doin' out there?" Rod called in a high-pitched voice that sounded off-key. "You still admiring that fourteen-pointer? C'm'on in. We's got us some company."

Moving slowly, as if his joints were stiff, Norm walked inside, blinking against the glare as he glanced about, concentrating on standing straight. It looked as he'd imagined. There were two girls, college or young working girls, he couldn't tell for sure. One of them, a tall, slender girl with straight brown hair and a long, thin face, sat on Merald's lap. The other girl sat on the arm of the easy chair beside Glenn, apparently trying to coax him into taking a fifty-dollar walk into the back room. She was short, well proportioned, almost plump. Her face was large, the bone structure solid, the skin smooth. When she looked at him her blue eyes were direct, judging him.

"Well, if we don't have a big one here," she said as Norm entered the living room. "I'm Sally."

Norm looked in her eyes, then quickly away.

"The big is all on the outside," Butch said with a loud laugh, his eyes squinting to see that Norm went along. "What you see is what you get."

Norm smiled and moved over to pour himself a stiff drink. Sally stood up and moved from Glenn over beside Norm. She looked up, her head barely even with his chest. "I'll take a drink. Brandy and water. Heavy on the brandy."

Norm nodded. He began to sweat, keenly aware of her perfume and her touching his elbow. He poured her drink, feeling her eyes boring into his back as he worked, the game in progress.

"What's your game?" Sally asked quietly.

Norm glanced up in surprise. He jerked his head sideways. "No game at all, lady. I'm just here to look at the stars."

Butch laughed. "And that, sweet Sally, is the pure truth. That's what Norman there does the best, stand outside and look at the stars. That and make up wild stories."

"There's nothing wrong with that," Sally said. "There's life out there, you know."

Thank you, Sally, Norm said to himself, and circled the sofa to put more wood in the fireplace.

"Looks like you've been tipping a few there, Norm," Rod said.

"I think everyone's been tipping a few."

"Not me," Glenn spoke up in a heavy voice. "When Bernie came around we started playing cribbage and behaved ourselves."

"Sounds like a hell of a lot of fun," Merald said, pleased with himself. Behind his rimless glasses his face was fixed in a grin. He had his arm inside the tall girl's sweater, rubbing her back. He introduced her to Norm as Patty. Norm glanced toward the back room, where David had been sent to bed. "The kid knows better than to say anything," Merald said thickly, reading the look. "Besides, he knows it doesn't matter."

"To you or him?"

"Why, you son of a bitch!" Merald pushed Patty from his lap and started to get up.

"Sit the fuck down, Merald," Butch yelled. "Let's not ruin this now. Norm, please keep your goddamn mouth shut unless you have something civil to say. You've more than filled your quota of troublemaking this week. Now, goddamn it, everyone drink up and be merry."

"Incidentally, Norm," Rod said, "my luck is still running good. You seen that blonde bombshell I met at the Silver Slipper. Whew, now she was something. Like a damn earthquake. Everything *moved*. I tell ya, she put Raquel Welch to shame." He winked. "And let me tell you, she knows how to use what I got—"

"Yeah, for ten minutes and a hundred bucks." Butch laughed. "You were gone before you came and don't even know it."

Rod's face turned red. "I was gone damn near an hour and you know it. And it wasn't a hundred dollars."

"The ninety-nine dollar quickie," Butch said. "The cold-cut discount."

"You've got to admit she was really something,"

Rod said. "And I scored, didn't I? That's what counts. Just like with the big black this aft—"

"Rod, I think you scored one other time today," Sally said. She glanced conspiratorially at Norm.

"How's that?" Rod asked.

"That 'blonde bombshell,' Cherry," Sally said. "She's a year 'round pro, up from Chicago for opening week of the deer season. I'd say you have crabs."

Guffaws resounded off the varnished log walls and through the rafters where wet boots and socks were stacked to dry and where the antlers hung quietly in their final resting place. Rod jumped to his feet, less handsome now that rage contorted his face. "I ought to bust you one in the mouth."

"Oh, but I thought that was my job," Sally said calmly. The others burst out with laughter again.

It looked as if Rod might go for her. "Sit down," Norm said, reaching out and straight-arming Rod backward onto the sofa, the force of his shove much harder than he'd intended. "Sorry, Rod. We just don't want to get anything started here."

"I'll get you something started, Norm," Rod screamed as he again jumped to his feet. "You just wait. I'll get you something started. You just can't stand it because I shot the big black—"

"That wasn't the big black." Norm was finally letting his voice rise too. Everyone in the room turned.

"Well, if that wasn't the big black, why don't you go out there and shoot the real son of a bitch and prove it to me—"

"Maybe I will."

"Yeah, sure."

"You better sit down and shut up, Norm," Butch said. "You've got everyone pissed enough the way it is. Taking my goddamn jeep and never saying a word. Some shack partner."

"That's for sure," Merald put in. He had another cigar clamped in the corner of his mouth. "You've been making trouble all damn weekend. Some hunting trip you're making for us."

Sally glanced at Patty, a warning. "I think we have to leave now."

"Hey, hold on, it's all right," Butch said with a laugh. "We just have something personal here. It won't affect you girls. Isn't that right, Norm?"

Norm waved his hand to dismiss the matter. He glanced about the room, taking them in, seeing Bernie huddled silently in a tattered easy chair off to one side. "How're you hanging, Bernie?"

Bernie looked barely able to lift his head. He shrugged. " 'S okay, Norm. Hanging in there." He resumed his fixation on the floor, then after a few moments suddenly brightened. He tried to whisper, his voice carrying. "Say, buddy, how about lending me fifty bucks?"

"Fifty bucks?"

"Yeah, fifty bucks." Bernie jerked his head toward the girls.

Out of the corner of his eye Norm could see Sally shaking her head, a plea and a warning. "I, ah, don't have that much on me, Bern. I spent more than I figured on tonight. . . ."

Bernie stared upward with his eyes watery. His voice became unusually hard. "So you're going to back away from me too?" He guzzled his drink, then suddenly thrust the glass toward Norm. "At least get me another drink . . . buddy."

"I'll get it," Sally said, stepping in front of Norm and taking the glass before Bernie could refuse. "One other thing, fellas. We like your party and everything, but it is getting late and if no one else is interested than we should be getting back to town." She paused to survey the room, her eyes coming last to Norm.

Norm stared into space across the room, the feeling deep in his loins, a feeling he despised, and that persisted.

"Butch, what about you? You good for one more?" Sally asked. A nervous tremor underlay her confident tone. Suddenly Norm understood, two amateurs trying to tough it out, trying to act as they imagined pros would.

"Hell, yes," Butch said. "I could go all night long. But not with you. At least, not at that price. Christ, my old lady would kill me" . . . uneasy grin . . . "especially if she knew what I had to pay."

"But otherwise she wouldn't give a damn, right?" Sally asked.

"Fuck no. It's the old story, what you don't know can't hurt you. And you listen, you little shit, we're paying you to fuck, not ask questions."

"Hey, watch it, Butch," Glenn said. He stood up and took Sally's elbow and guided her away from Butch. "You better watch yourself," he said quietly to the girl. "Butch has a temper. He could blow. We don't need any trouble around here."

Patty looked as if she was about to panic. She pulled away from Merald and got up.

"Hey," Glenn said. "We're not going to hurt anyone. If you want to go now, I'll drive you back to town."

"It's all right, Patty," Sally said sharply. "Nothing's going to happen. We can leave when we want to. If no one else wants us around, we can go."

"I would say no one here will be using your services anymore tonight, young ladies," Butch said with elaborate politeness. He smiled, his anger apparently a thing of the past. "Besides, everyone who's left is either broke like Bernie, too old and uptight like Norm there, or full of his own novocaine like doc. The only other trooper we have is young David in yonder, and he's only a lad of fourteen." Butch grinned suddenly. "Merald, I'd say it's time you devirginized that kid of yours."

"Hell no," Merald said. He heaved his bulk out of

the easy chair, staggered sideways until he gained the support of a wall.

"Hell, they'll do it for free," Butch continued in his thick voice. "These girls would like nothing better than to break in a virgin kid. Wouldn't you, girls?"

"For thirty dollars, sure," Sally said. "Patty won't mind." She looked at her partner to reassure her.

"Yeah," Rod said. "First the old man on the ride back in the jeep and then his virgin kid. It'd be great."

"That'll get the headlines in the *Tribune*." Butch laughed.

"I ain't sending any slut in there with David," Merald said, his cigar tumbling down his chest to the floor. He wiped at his heavy, unshaved face with the back of his hand.

" 'Slut'?" Patty said, voice rising. "You fat slob. You look at yourself lately?"

"Why, you skinny bitch," Merald said and lumbered forward. Patty circled behind the sofa.

"Hey, hey," Butch said. Still laughing, he grabbed Merald, both men dropping their drinks in the process. But Merald wouldn't be deterred and the two men, each of them weighing over two hundred and fifty pounds, began to wrestle, giant bears hugging each other, swaying to and fro, Butch laughing, Merald cursing. The others in the room came to their feet, ready to move out of the way, circling to stay clear of the action.

David appeared in the bunkroom door, a fat little boy in baggy thermal underwear, his black curly hair tousled. In the center of the room the two bears struggled in the dancing light of the fireplace, grunting and cursing, swaying back and forth as if moved by a powerful wind. Suddenly, like a huge pine tree snapping in two, they toppled sideways, splintering a chair and rolling over the sofa and up against the wall.

"Goddamnit, Norm, get the fuck over here and help me hold this bastard down before I have to cold-cock him," Butch grunted as he strained to catch his breath.

To Norm the room was a merry-go-round of lights and noise, bodies all over the place, the girl, Patty, almost hysterical; Sally still calm, whispering earnestly in Patty's ear; Glenn leaning against a wall, watching with the same disinterest he viewed television; Bernie back behind the kitchen counter for safety, trying to stand up straight; Rod jumping up and down and circling the two fat bears like a little kid watching a schoolyard fight. Norm picked his way across the room, around fallen chairs and the overturned sofa, kicking an unseen glass across the floor. His shadow loomed from the light of the fireplace and the single lamp. Rod was loving it. "Man oh man, have you ever seen such a circus in your damn life? This is great."

Norm ignored Rod's "Let 'em go," loomed over the two fat bears and paused.

"Well, move, ya fucker," Butch said, between gasps. Merald had stopped struggling.

"Le's break it up," Norm said. He grabbed the back of Merald's shirt with both hands and heaved him backward, getting a grip on one arm as Butch struggled to his feet and seized the other.

"Now goddamnit, Merald, settle down or I'm going to have to deck you." Butch was completely winded.

"Okay, okay," Merald said, laughing as he gasped to catch his breath.

"Dammit, Merald, the kid can do it," Butch argued. "Hell, he's fourteen. How old were you the first time you got hold of some pussy?"

"Twelve. Some eighteen-year-old dropout got her twat on me one afternoon down at Lindbergh Park." Merald laughed at the memory. "Ah, fuck"—he pulled away from Norm—"David, you want this girl here should come visit you for a while?"

David glanced around the room, watching all the eyes focused in his direction. He swallowed, trying not to look at Rod's leering grin. "Ah, I don't know, dad. It . . . it doesn't matter."

"Yes or no. Decide."

"Ah, yeah, I suppose."

"Atta boy," his father said. "Go ahead," he growled toward the tall, slender girl who, after whispering fiercely with Sally, reluctantly crossed the room, circling wide of Merald. "And no funny crap, either," Merald snapped, thrusting his forefinger at her.

"We need the money first," Sally said. "Pay in advance, you know."

"Money-grabbing bitches," Merald said. He reached in his pocket and threw some bills on the floor. "There, take your filthy money."

"The law of supply and demand," Sally said with a tight smile.

"Ah," and Merald waved his hand as if to dismiss her. He turned and almost bumped into Norm, who was still standing in the middle of the room, not too steady himself. "And you, Norm," Merald growled, pushing his face up toward Norm's. "If you ever lay a hand on me again it'll be the last hand you ever lay on anyone. Got that?"

"Ummm," Norm grunted as if he hadn't heard. He brushed past Merald and went to the kitchen table and poured himself a water glass half full of straight whiskey. Abruptly, as if out of thin air, a soft, warm body pressed up against his side, turning him and pushing into his stomach and chest. A hand crept inside his shirt, pressing against the fire of his flesh.

"Mmmm, you're hot," Sally said softly, her voice low so the others couldn't hear. "They call you Norm, right? The way things look to me, Norm, except for the dentist over there, you're the only one around here with any sense. How'd you ever hook up with these guys?"

Norm laughed. Joannie's question. He laughed some more, unusual for him, barely able to control himself, a man verging on tears.

Sally glanced up, puzzled, her hand working inside his shirt, dipping down beneath his belt. Norm stiffened, stomach taut.

"That Merald is pretty nervous, isn't he?" Sally asked. "He doesn't even like his own son. If you ask me he's dangerous, just like Butch when he loses his temper. He's out of control."

"Dangerous? Too tied up. Everybody's dangerous. Even me."

"I can't believe that," Sally said. She worked her other hand up inside his shirt. "You're so warm, Norm. C'm on. Let's take a walk into the other bedroom. You want to, don't you?"

"No," he said hastily. "I can't, I'm married." He pushed down at her shoulders, gently trying to pull away.

"Easy, Norm. Don't panic now. Look, we don't have to do it." She leaned close, ignoring the others in the living room sitting around the fireplace drinking and talking, laughing about the boy David. "When's the last time you had a blow job?" she asked, her voice soft.

"Ah . . ." Norm tried to laugh. "I don't know." But he thought, never, never in his whole life. Now?

He realized that the top of his pants was unbuttoned, her hand was inside his fly, touching ever so gently, a fleeting touch against a prick that felt as big and solid as his forearm. A blow job, the one thing Joannie had never brought herself to do.

The hand withdrew and slipped into his own, pulling him gently toward the back bunkroom. No, he thought, feeling his hardness. Still . . . Joannie wouldn't mind, hell, she didn't really care . . . he just wanted her to . . . He followed the girl.

"Hey, the Norman's going in the back room," Rod yelped. "At least you'll score with *something* today, Norm. Make her earn it."

"Don't kiss her or you might get a taste of my cock," Butch called out.

"Screw them," Sally muttered, as he looked back. She snapped on the bright overhead light and closed the door, the Sheetrock partition barely muffling the talk and laughter from the living room. She blinked in the glare, a girl of twenty-two or so, Norm thought, not that much older than his Kim. "I'll need to have the money firs'," she said.

She's drunk. He glanced at the glazed film of her eyes. She knows what she's doing, though. He held out his wallet and watched while she picked out three twenties and stuffed them into the pocket of her brown slacks, stretched so taut on her soft, heavily rounded buttocks. She reached past him and snapped off the light. "Come," she whispered and led him over to the window beside one bunk.

She pressed against him, her hands inside his shirt caressing his back, a long smooth stroke that brought his flesh alive. He held her shoulders, feeling the frailty of her in his large hands, holding her as though to keep her away, a girl less than half his age and little more than half his size.

The top of his pants came open and his shorts and pants dropped together, exposing his hardness to the cold air of the room. She knelt. The tips of her touching fingers vibrated his cock. Her lips touched lightly on the flesh of his stomach. A blow job . . . a young girl going about her job, taking his cock into the dampness of her mouth, something he'd dreamed about for too long, an act she'd forget about by morning. . . .

He sank his hands into her short brown hair, surging, his head turned upward staring out the window at the brilliant sheen of stars. "No . . . Joannie, Joannie," he grunted half aloud. But it was too late. It was done.

CHAPTER XIII

It was the way Norm looked when he went into the back bunkroom with Sally, Glenn thought. He swore softly. Norm had seemed to make a point of looking directly back at him, brown eyes mocking, challenging, showing off his virility by openly taking the girl in front of them. He got to his feet, glaring at the closed door Norm had retreated behind.

He paced across the living room and poured himself a stiff drink, driving his hand to touch the bulge of the gun beneath his belt. If Norm had told the cops after they separated in town, where were they? And if he didn't tell them, why not? Because there was no body? Then it must have been Norm he'd fired on . . . and missed. But a body went down. . . .

He drifted in back of the others sitting around the fireplace laughing and drinking and paused beneath the gun rack. He reached and caressed the smooth finish of his rifle stock, seeing himself taking the rifle off the rack, cradling it in his hands . . . Then the others' uncomprehending surprise, the frantic slow-motion rush to escape the thunder of his bucking weapon, bodies slamming backward and tumbling to the floor, the amazement in the proximity of death. . . .

For several long seconds Glenn dared not move, the thrashing in his chest so loud he was sure it could be heard. He shook his head, tried to loosen the knot in his stomach. Norm was good, more than the others imagined. He thought of the back room where the tall one was showing young David how to go with the pull of his cock, to where Norm and the short plump one rolled their sweaty ugly bodies together like two pigs in heat.

Him and Norm.

Glenn managed a smile, seeing himself striding slowly out into the dusty street, pants tight, the firm touch and oily smell of leather holding him together, the big .45 cailber iron weighing at his hip. And down the street tall, homely Norm stepping out from an alley, the butt of his pistol jutting outward, framed against the bright blue sky. So casual, so cool they were, the onlookers would think. And yet one of them would die soon. . . .

Once again, as he had so often before, he reviewed the scenario. Get Norm alone and end it. They wouldn't believe he did it on purpose. Even if they put him on trial. And he knew he wouldn't break. He'd demonstrated that he could maintain control, especially when they watched. A man doing killings like that had to be insane, everyone knew that. There'd be no hard evidence, no motive—no case. The accused was a victim of circumstances. . . . "Take a look, ladies and gentlemen," the defense attorney would say, and he would look at them calmly, the good father, the good provider, the good husband. He did his job well, he treated his employees fairly, with respect. . . . He went to church with Barbara and the kids every Sunday, he didn't smoke, he hardly ever drank, he belonged to the Lions Club and jogged at the YMCA. He didn't cheat on his

wife. People respected him. . . . "Yes, ladies and
gentlemen, we have established that there had been
three other hunters shot within thirty miles of this
same area, and it's even possible that the late Norman Petrie was hit by a stray bullet from the defendant's rifle. As we all know, he did shoot at a buck in
there. But *there is no motive. None.* The record of
the defendant speaks for itself. He happened to be in
the area where someone was accidentally shot. The
worst we have here is an accident. We have heard circumstances and circumstances, but not *one* bit of
hard evidence. Ladies and gentlemen, I ask you to
look at the defendant and judge for yourself. Look
for yourselves at an innocent man." . . . "Thank
you," Glenn heard himself saying as he stood to re-
ceive his not guilty verdict and walk calmly away
with Barbara and Rachel and Glenn III, Glenn Sr.
hobbling over with tears in his eyes to give him a
hug. "You should sue," Glenn Sr. was saying. . . .
"No," he would say generously. "They made a mistake, we'll let it be. . . ."

He strode into the shack kitchen to freshen his
drink, then went and sat with the others until the
girls came out of the back rooms, first Sally, and then
the other, Patty. He watched them carefully. His eyes
dropped to the rise and fall of Sally's large breasts
beneath her sweater, to the curve of her hips, to the
hollow of her crotch where minutes before Norm had
been. He breathed more quickly, feeling her naked
breasts with his lips, feeling himself rise, a pressure, a
pain, a release he craved with all his might. His eyes
moved as the two girls moved, unaccountably rising
up to focus on their necks, long necks, vulnerable
necks.

Suddenly he stood—they needed a ride back to
town.

"I'll take you," he heard himself say. He looked at
Sally, the one who had gone back with Norm. In his

mind, the naked hardness of himself stood out in the winter air, he seized her by her mane of hair, driving her to her knees, both hands pushing her face at his hardness, rising, suddenly tossing her naked body back and climbing up over her, towering far above as he drove himself deep inside her, just as he'd towered over those others in the forest. A giggle bubbled behind his clenched teeth. They couldn't know but they'd find out, his cock was just as powerful as his rifle. He'd show them. . . .

"Let's go," he said calmly, focusing on the thinness of their necks. The pressure at his crotch moved upward, commanding every nerve. "Let's go," he managed to say, touching to feel the hunting knife on his belt. "It's a damn long ways back to town. Especially at night."

CHAPTER XIV

His eyes opened and where once he'd felt nothing he became filled with pain. The shack was dark, dawn a half hour away according to the luminous dial of his watch. The sound of snoring carried from the bunkrooms, a freight train of noise that echoed through a room sour with the odor of smoke and booze and sweaty clothes. He closed his eyes and lay back, aware now of everything that had happened.

Suddenly he grunted and threw the covers onto the floor. The snorers paused, turning, smacking their lips before resuming their sawmill in concert. Norm clambered to his feet, swayed back and forth, was hit by a dizziness that almost drove him to his knees. He shook his head, then set about feeling for his clothes, unable for the moment to recall the layout of the room. Two pairs of socks, wool pants over his long underwear, a wool shirt, boots, the black-and-red-checkered wool jacket, his hat, his rifle, a handful of shells. Now he could move. He made for the door a bit too quickly, kicking an unseen chair across the floor, ignoring the grunts behind him, pushing out the door into the cold darkness of pre-dawn.

Both jeeps were back. Glenn had returned from

taking the two girls back to town and he hadn't even heard. He'd been that far gone, he thought, feeling it was sort of a justification. But it really was a lie, he knew, as he staggered on away from the shack, pausing at the deer-hanging pole to stare at the dark outline of Rod's fourteen-pointer. The beauty, the magnificence, all lost. Nothing left but a lifeless hunk of meat, cold stiff meat. The deer had jumped wrong. And because of that Rod was the best? Norm winced, turned away.

It was daylight by the time he reached the point in the seven-mile swamp he'd been aiming for. He paused, the sweat running freely down the small of his back and the insides of his biceps. He reached into his pocket and loaded his rifle, one bullet in the chamber, one in the magazine, all he'd need.

He went to work, looking around, taking in the sky, the ridge, the direction of the wind, a check of his senses before he stepped out, cutting down into the almost impassable thickets of tag alders and marsh grass and potholes covered with thin slush ice. He was aware of everything that had happened and of what he was going to do, had to do. . . .

At first he made no attempt at stealth, ducking, jumping from one clump of moss and marsh grass to another, noisily sweeping aside branches of tag alders that blocked his path. Several times he paused to catch his breath, thinking on his plan, the need to pace himself. . . .

By eight o'clock he'd covered almost two miles, his movement out from the ridge like a huge fishhook so he was now heading back toward the ridge at a point a good half mile down from where he'd first entered the swamp. He paused, his heart pounding at the walls of his chest, his body bathed in sweat, feet soaking wet from having crashed through slush ice on too many potholes. He'd stuffed his hat into his pocket. His black hair was thick and snarled, peppered with bits of dirt and bark from his rush through the swamp. He rubbed at the dampness covering his long face, feeling the coarseness, the solidity he'd once allowed himself to think of as strength. His brown eyes flickered over the tangle of forest inches from his face. He glanced up at the blue sky with its scattered clouds. Snow was coming, tonight, tomorrow, he couldn't be certain. He bunched up some fresh snow and chewed on it for water. A half mile more of swamp, he thought. It couldn't be done, they'd say, and he almost felt that way himself. He spat hard to clear his throat and set out through the swamp, gradually slowing his pace and cutting down the amount of noise he made.

Periodically he crossed small clearings of marsh grass from which he could see ahead to the distant ridge and to a dark green cluster of hemlocks growing out of the swamp between himself and the ridge. When he was about three hundred yards away he began his stalk in earnest, a stalk such as he hadn't attempted in years.

Staring into the thickets ahead, he felt the near impossibility of his task. One miscue would ruin it . . . one snap of a twig, one slip of a foot through slush ice, one scrape of a branch against another. The slightest sound would give him away. Because of the tangles and clumps of grass and the interlocking puddles of swamp water and the thick branches of tag alders, he'd have to be hunched over, almost stooping, zigzagging back and forth to find the best path, crawling on hands and knees at times. And never make a sound.

He closed his eyes, resting, trying to ignore thoughts of what was to come, knowing only what had to be done—strip Rod of an honor he defiled, and draw out whoever it was who'd fired at him in the creek. Could they be linked? He thought so.

One by one he had reviewed the others—Butch,

Merald, Rod, Glenn and Bernie, seeing them individually, rejecting most of them one by one. But as a group, as hunters in a shack, the possibilities were clearer. He grunted, a sound of satisfaction. When Rod . . . when the killer woke up and saw he was gone, and then when he came back and threw what by then he would have done in the man's face . . . the man would have to move then, Norm thought.

Have to.

He set out through the swamp.

Long after Norm had made his pre-dawn departure, the others woke up in the gloom of the shack. They shuffled slowly about beneath the rafters of antlers, blinking at the daylight when the curtains were drawn back, trying to get their bearings, drinking juice and coffee, popping Rolaids and aspirin.

Butch smirked when young David emerged, the boy's black hair matted, his thermal underwear baggy even on his pudgy frame. "Well, damn, if it isn't the big stud. You had that gal in there over a half hour, didn't you, kid? What'd you do, fuck her brains out?"

"Two or three times, I'll bet," Rod said with a laugh.

"Some year for a fourteen-year-old," Butch said. "A spike buck, your first broad. Damn. Some year."

David grinned sheepishly, with pride.

"You better take it easy, David. You're outdoing yer old man. You're going to make him jealous."

"That'll be the day," Merald said, not looking at his son.

"Have I got a headache," Glenn complained, the last of them to get up.

"You should practice up more during the year," Butch said. "Look at Bernie there. He drank twice as much as you, passed out twice and he's raring to go. Ain't so, Bern?"

Bernie slowly turned his bloodshot, purple-blue

eyes toward Butch. His face sagged beneath the gray stubble of whiskers. He rubbed at his large bumpy nose. "When you get ready to go, Butch, I'll be there. You can bet your ass on that."

Butch wrapped his arm around Bernie's shoulders. "Ah, good ole Bernie, never say die."

Bernie nodded, pleased with what he considered a show of affection.

"Hey, you talk about raring to go, I'm ready for another fourteen-pointer," Rod yelled. He jumped high, seizing a rafter and pumping out a fast series of fifteen pullups, eyes riveted on the beam as he worked. He dropped to the floor, carefully holding his breath in check. "All day in the woods, a fourteen-pointer, women, booze, deer, out all night. C'm'on, I'm ready to give 'er again."

"What should we do, Butch?" Merald asked, ignoring Rod's show.

"Well, I could see a little road hunting," Butch said. "After last night I'm a wee bit pooped. These old legs aren't what they used to be. We could drive up toward the slashings and maybe make a couple of short drives in there where those forties are squared off."

"What about Norm?" Glenn asked. "He must be out hunting already."

"Yeah, and that's what gets me about this whole deal," Butch said. "Norm just isn't acting normal."

"What do you mean?" Merald asked. "Norm always gets up and gets out before daylight. Every single day of the season he's out there like this."

"Yeah, but after everything he claims has happened, he gets up and goes out hunting just like normal? Uh huh, it doesn't make sense."

"I think that fourteen-pointer of mine really got to him," Rod said.

"You and that goddamn fourteen-pointer are starting to get to *me*," Butch said. "Let's get out of here and go hunting."

"I think I'll just stick around here," Glenn said, taking a deep breath. "I'm not feeling so hot."

"Hey, goddamnit," Butch said, "you said that yesterday morning. The least you can do is help us get our bucks. What the fuck?"

Glenn's face reddened, he nodded meekly.

They took the two jeeps out into the back logging roads, using their CB radios to keep pace with each other.

Once two deer crossed in front of Rod's jeep and stopped back in the trees, still visible. Rod eased the jeep to a stop as Bernie frantically jerked the case off his rifle and thrust a bullet into the chamber. Quickly he poked the rifle out of the rolled-down window, Glenn watching to see that no cars were coming that might catch them in the act of shooting from a vehicle.

"It's a godamn buck," Rod said in an excited whisper. "Shoot, Bernie. Christ. He's going to run."

Bernie's gun went off.

"Ya missed, ya missed," Rod screamed. "A standing shot, a lousy hundred feet . . . goddammit, Bernie—"

"I . . . I couldn't see good."

"That thing was wide open."

"We better check for blood," Glenn said, pushing to get out of the back seat.

"We've got to get out of here," Rod said, glancing back down the road. "That thing wasn't hit. He didn't even flinch."

"You can never tell," Glenn said, "it's best to be certain. Case your gun, Bern. I'll be right back."

"He wasn't hit, I tell ya," Rod said, but Glenn was already out and wading through the snow.

"No blood," Glenn said a few minutes later when he returned, a fact Rod broadcast over the CB, along with the information that Bernie had just missed a standing, broadside shot at a nice spike.

"Ah, tell Bern to open his eyes next time," Butch called back over the CB.

"Next time he'll be in the back seat," Rod called back. "Or maybe next time we'll get him a machine gun."

"How about a mortar," Merald said over Butch's radio and they all laughed and drove on, peering intently into the forest. Bernie huddled down against the side of the jeep, head and eyes turned out toward the forest. He held two rifle shells in his hand, rolling them over and over, clicking them together.

It took Norm forty-five minutes to cover the first hundred yards toward the hemlock island and over an hour for the next hundred. The last hundred seemed to take forever.

By the time he was fifty yards away from the tiny island of hemlocks he'd literally slowed to a crawl, frequently dropping to his hands and knees and threading his way through a tiny teepee-like opening left by the interlocking tangles of black tag alders. He breathed gently as he moved, twisting his shoulders sideways to slip through a tiny opening, lifting his hand and rifle and gently getting a sound footing on a clump of grass, turning on his side, watching behind him as he pulled his knee in under his belly to miss a branch, then shifting his weight slowly, noiselessly onto a resting place and searching ahead for his next move. Several times he simply lay in the small canyon between clumps of alders, his head and rifle resting in the cradle of his arms. He'd close his eyes and reach out and suck the moisture from a handful of snow, his heart banging. He was wet to his skin from head to foot with sweat, melted snow and swamp water that began to freeze and chill his every aching muscle within minutes after each stop. When the chills shook his body he'd pick up and move on, sometimes, if the brush permitted, standing and moving at a crouch, sometimes forced back to his hands and knees.

At times dull agony of muscles held too long in isometric tension became so great that he almost screamed. Once, in the midst of exhausted agony, he imagined himself from the viewpoint of a bird, a tiny figure in red and black crawling through the center of a huge, lifeless swamp.

At last he reached the small island of hemlocks. A new alertness came to him with a surge of adrenalin that washed away his agony and exhaustion. Slowly he picked his head up, his eyes taking in every thicket, every shadow, every hollow. His head cocked to pick up the slightest sound, he worked his way through the scrub balsam on the edge of the island. Once a tiny twig caught on his hip and snapped like a firecracker. He froze, holding his breath and listening. The noise hadn't been that loud, he knew, but it was there, a sound out of the ordinary. For five full minutes he did not move. The deep chill had him shivering. Still he did not move. Animals knew the finality of death. They faced it every day, they saw it all around them, life and death. Patience was easy by comparison.

He resumed his crawl up the side of the small rise on the outer edge of the island, the sound of his movements muffled by the carpet of pine needles and thin covering of snow. Moving his head so slowly that it would appear there was no movement at all, he peered over the crest of the incline to survey the flat of the island.

It was larger than it had looked from the swamp. It ran at least a hundred feet in length, ringed by scrub balsam around the edges, sunk in the middle and at the edge toward the distant highland, thick with tall spreading hemlocks in the low areas, and almost completely free of underbrush. Without moving his head, his eyes searched each thicket, each dark shape of a fallen tree or an old stump. Down low like this, the noise of the wind muffled by the hemlock, he could see everything but the far end of the island. And he saw nothing.

He swallowed against a dryness gluing his throat together. His muscles shook, jelly without strength. Nothing. He saw nothing at all.

After a few minutes he managed to calm his panic. It wasn't over yet. There was one last chance, hope—the small neck jutting out toward the mainland.

Slowly, he resumed his crawl forward on hands and knees, the pain of every move jabbing straight to his brain. His knees were swollen, raw, getting too painful to handle his weight. It was probably pointless now, but he kept going.

He could have stood up. The terrain was open enough to permit silent movement. But then the silhouette of his movement could be seen that much farther. Never mind pain and exhaustion, he couldn't take the chance.

By late morning the others, weary of driving, swung down the blacktop town road that led past Swede's backwoods tavern and stopped in for a beer and a hamburger.

Even though it was only mid-morning the tavern was lined with hunters. "Hey, there's the Trail's End boys," Swede called as they shuffled into the room. "Those are the guys I was telling you about," he said to the people at the bar. "A spike, an eight-pointer, and a *fourteen*-pointer. Any more, fellas?"

"Nope, we've been dogging it," Butch said.

"Everyone having the usual?"

"Yeah," Butch replied. He crowded in with the others at one end of the L-shaped bar. "And give us that dice box. I feel the call to rip the boys for a few bucks."

"Hey, Swede, where're you keeping the women these days?" Rod asked with a laugh. "We're getting a little shack-happy out there."

Swede laughed. "Back room as usual, Rodney. Only the price has gone up and you'll have to wait in line. Indian gals are popular these days."

"Smoked meat, huh?" Merald said. "You touch that, Rod, and you can figure on staying away from the old lady for a few weeks."

"Go ahead on back, Rod," Butch laughed. "Fifty bucks will get you a knothole and some fresh liver."

"Who said anything about fresh," Swede said as he mixed a lineup of drinks. He glanced up and down the bar, then whispered in conspiratorial fashion so they all could hear. "Truth of the matter is, I've been put out of business. When Butch went backroom the other day I found out afterward he done ate the liver." Uproarious laughter.

"Not bad flavor either," Butch said, "though maybe a tad on the chewy side."

"So you're out of business then, Swede?" Bernie asked.

"Temporarily," Swede said. "Unless you can find a volunteer, tonight you'll have to keep your pride in your pants."

"What you should do, Swede, is hire some queer's asshole," Butch said.

"That and a bottle of vaseline," Rod said. The line of men crowding the dark mahogany bar laughed, some of it forced.

"Looks like a nice day," Swede said, nodding toward the bright sunshine glaring off the snow and the relatively warm twenty-degree temperature.

"Better here than being cooped up in the city, that's for sure," Glenn replied, reminding himself of the importance of acting normal, one of the boys. "Course, almost anything's better than that."

"Amen, Glenn brother," Swede said. "I spent twenty years busting my ass in Milwaukee breweries. Lived on the south side with all those colored. Pure hell from dawn till dusk. You could castrate me before I'd move back there."

"I don't think I'd pay that price for anything," Rod said, and laughed. "It's good to get away, but me, I like the action . . . city sights, city lights, it's always moving. And besides, that's where the money's at."

"To each his own," Swede said over his shoulder as he moved down the bar. When he returned he tossed a newspaper down on the bar. "You guys seen this? They found another dead hunter last night down by the old dynamite shack area, third one in four years and all of 'em within twenty-five miles of here. . . . The third one and they don't know what happened. . . ."

The men stared, not speaking, dry clucking sounds coming from Bernie's bobbing throat. Their eyes found the headline: THIRD HUNTER SLAIN IN FOUR YEARS. "The law's on this with every man they've got," Swede said. "I imagine they'll be out your way sooner or later asking questions. There's no proof, but one theory goes that some guy has been doing these on purpose."

They stared, their silence bringing a puzzled twisting to Swede's dark eyes. "Well, what's with you guys? What do you think?"

Huh?" Merald.

"Think?" Butch. "Ah, what's to think? I mean it seems hard to believe, I figure it's just coincidence of stray bullets, maybe guys not wearing their orange gear. . . ."

"That's the thing," Swede said, "it *is* hard to believe. That's why I think one guy is doing it. Year after year. These aren't strays. No way. They've all been right in the back or the chest."

So it wasn't Norm. . . . "If one guy was doing all these he'd have to be crazy, a psychopath," Glenn said knowingly. "Over three or four years, he'd surely give himself away, wouldn't he? I mean, at least the guys he hunts with would spot him."

"Maybe just the opposite," Swede said, wiping the bar. "People get so used to being with a guy they don't really notice when he changes. Besides, you'd never believe something like this about someone you'd known personally for years. It wouldn't seem possible. And that's what would fool you."

"But could a psychopath go on four years and nobody notice?" Glenn asked Swede.

"Seems unlikely, I admit. Except the guy could be a loner. . . . Besides, pick up the newspaper these days. Guys in Texas, California, New York, killing and burying dozens of victims for years and years before they're caught. No one they know notices them. When it comes to people, I figure anything's possible."

"It's sick all right," Merald said.

"Do they have any proof that it's one guy?" Glenn asked, reaching for the newspaper.

"They're not saying, but I think there's damn little," Swede said. "In most cases the bullet went clean through the body. There's no witnesses, not even any tracks in the snow. This last one was shot during that little snowstorm yesterday. The only reason they found him last night was because his brother knew the stand he was on." Swede moved to the other end of the bar to fill a glass.

Merald leaned forward. "Goddamn! What are we going to do now?" he said, fumbling to get one of his huge cigars unwrapped and into his mouth.

"We should have gone to the law when Norm said

he found that body," Glenn said. "I told you so. It would have been best, safest."

"Yeah, but who the hell believed he was telling the truth," Butch argued. "We didn't know."

"If they find out we knew about that body and didn't report it we're in one hell of a lot of trouble," Merald went on in a high voice, leaning heavily in toward the others, squeezing Bernie over against Butch. "This'll ruin me."

"They'll blame all of us," Bernie said, eyes fixed on the bar. "All of us."

"Yeah, but you don't have anything to lose," Merald said.

"Whatdaya mean?"

"Settle down, goddamnit," Butch said.

"What are we going to do?" Merald asked.

"How the fuck should I know, nothing. Same as before."

"I think someone *is* intentionally shooting people," Bernie abruptly said. He crooked his finger and pointed it down the bar. "Kablam. Right in the back. Don't forget what happened to Norm Saturday—"

"Knock it off, Bernie," Butch said, and took hold of Bernie's elbow in a tight grip.

"What about the cops?" Merald whispered. "We have to go to the cops—"

"What the hell for?" Rod said. "They've already found the body. We couldn't tell them anything they don't know. So why hassle ourselves?"

"I think he's right," Glenn said. "They'd have to have something to look good—"

"And we'd be it," Rod said.

Butch looked sideways at Glenn, appraising him. "What the hell changed your mind? Yesterday you were as hot as fresh shit to go to the law."

"It's too late now," Glenn said. "If we'd gone right away it would have looked all right. But now . . . I think we're liable for failing to report it."

Butch lowered his large head, considering it all, his neck bulging above the back of his wool shirt. "Maybe we could forget it," he said softly, "and if it got down to where we were in a bind we could blame the whole thing on Norm, say we didn't see the body ourselves, which is true . . . that he didn't say or we didn't believe him. Hell, he's the only one that saw it anyhow, and *he* was the one that didn't report it. It's his neck, not ours."

"By damn, that's right." Rod smiled, proud of his calm. "I don't know what you guys are getting so up tight about anyhow. If the law comes around, give 'em old Norm. He's the one stirring up the whole thing. They're not going to mess with all of us. You know, it'd do old Norm some good to be taken over the coals. You know how damn careful he is to obey the law, always telling you what's right and wrong like he's a judge or something. . . ."

"Won't even drive over fifty-five." Butch took it up.

"Shh," Merald cautioned as Swede returned.

"You guys been doing any hunting out away from the shack?" Swede asked casually.

"Not much," Butch told him. "We did some road hunting this morning and saw a couple of flags. We've had all our luck around the shack so I think that's where we'll stick."

"Saw old Norm in here last night. Said you'd all been up to Hurley. How's the action?"

"Va-va voom!" Rod said, relieved that he'd changed the subject to his favorite one. "There's a blonde up there that's walking bowlegged this morning, I'll tell you that."

"She was bowlegged when ya met her," Butch said. "That's the only kind you mess around with any-how—"

"Well, what do you call yourself? Messing around with that jailbait—"

"That broad was crowding thirty."

"Shit, they were both minors."

"Whoa," Swede said, holding up his hand, his eyes showing puzzlement at the outburst. "I didn't mean to pry or anything, it's none of my G.D. business . . . here, have one on me." He busied himself setting up a line of beers, then moved down the bar to tend to his other customers. Once he glanced back over his shoulder.

"If you ever wise off like that again, Rod, I'll bust you right in the balls," Butch said, voice low and tight.

"It's your privilege to try—"

Glenn reached out and tapped Butch's clenching fist. "Not here, Butch, we can't afford the damn attention." Glenn's soft brown eyes looked earnest, his words sounded sensible.

"Yeah, I reckon," Butch muttered.

"The thing we do have to worry about," Doc continued, "is Norm. If the cops press him he might come up with that story about being shot at."

"Yeah, don't forget about that," Merald said.

"I ain't forgetting about anything," Butch said. "If Norm did get shot at he's taking it pretty goddamn calm. The guy pisses me off. . . . he even went out hunting this morning. Can you beat that? And what the hell for? He won't shoot a buck if he sees one anyhow."

"At least they'll have us all over the news," Bernie mumbled as he downed his beer. "Might be all right. You know, all that publicity, might not be so bad—"

"Son of a bitch, Bernie, don't get nuts like Norm," Merald said. "And why don't you take it easy on the booze for a while?"

"Get away . . ." Bernie threw off Merald's hand, clutching his drink to his chest and whirling away to protect the glass with his body.

"Dammit, settle *down*," Butch whispered. "Swede's already wondering what's going on. No more talk, we'll stonewall it. With the snowstorm out there that day, the cops can't prove anything . . ."

"What about Norm?" Glenn asked. "You know how he's been lately, he may not play along—"

"He'll play along," Butch said softly. "He'll play along or else."

"Or else what?" Rod said, blue eyes intense.

"When we leave we'll go back and hunt around the shack," Butch decided, ignoring Rod. "Everyone. Out driving around, the cops might stop us for questioning, And, if they drop by the shack during the day, no one will be there."

"And you *know* they won't be working at night, so no problem there," Rod said.

"All right then," Butch said, "the matter's settled. I'll take care of Norm. Now the less said the better."

"There's just one thing," Merald said, "*was* Norm shot at? And who *has* been doing all these killings? Are they strays, or do you think it could be murder?"

"Ah, I doubt it," Butch said, and waved his hand, as if trying to make the thought go away.

For a long while they sat in silence, chewing on their fat juicy hamburgers and raw onions and gulping their beer, engrossed in the art of eating, their thoughts on the possibility of murder . . . and a murderer—unknown, and just maybe . . . maybe one of them . . . ? They had come in talking and joking and laughing, they were silent now, refusing to look at one another or speak, tumbling deeper and deeper into their silence and the frightening thought that was unthinkable.

Norm moved in an animal trance, a panther stalking prey, aware only of the forest, of the snow and the way the trunks of the hemlock trees reached out of the earth, of the quiet carpet of snow and moss and flat pine needles beneath his hand and knees. He carried the old Winchester carefully, pausing to brush away the snow, setting it down gently, watching his every move and the ground ahead.

He spotted the buck long after he should have, in a part of the forest that abruptly stood out from the rest. It lay curled between the roots and trunks of two large hemlocks, its back to him, its head and towering antlers high, facing the distant mainland from which the sound of guns always came. The head was cocked, the ears moving back and forth, as if aware of some change in the forest but not sure what.

"The big black," Norm whispered.

Slowly, very slowly, he eased himself flat to lie in a soft bed of tiny three-inch moss trees. Gently, using thumb and forefinger so there would be no click, he eased off the safety, then raised the rifle to his shoulder, his movements slow, frozen each time the buck turned its head and the huge black antlers.

Once the buck turned its head completely back in his direction. Norm froze, squinted to cut down the glint of moisture in his eyes and the movement of a blink, every muscle stilled, the gentle breeze in his face as he'd intended. Being color blind the buck could not sense his unnatural color. But one movement, the tiniest suspicion, and the buck would be gone with one jump into the tangled swamp.

He could see the large brown eyes of the buck clearly, could sense the puzzlement as they examined his form, at the new log with the limb thrust out in front. Why hadn't that been noticed before? Several times the buck looked away, then quickly back, testing.

Five minutes . . . ten minutes, Norm couldn't say how long. He only knew the pain in tired muscles forced to hold unnatural positions as he lay cocked sideways with most of his weight resting on his sore left elbow. His left bicep quivered but he would not move. The ultimate test came now, face to face, with patience and the knowledge of what was required to ensure the kill. He must not fail.

After a long time the buck turned away. It looked for all the world like a deliberate move to ignore death fears inspired by a mere log. It was foolish.

Gently, Norm settled down on his stomach, peering through the circle under his scope and bringing the back vee and front bead in line, sliding the entire picture to the back of the big black's head. He took up the trigger slack.

A strange tremor went through his body. Forcibly he stilled the slight quivering of his arm. His gaze steadied, his finger tightened.

"God," he whispered, looking with both eyes over the top of his rifle. Such a magnificent creature, one of a kind, hunted by hundreds of men who slashed down the forests, used powerful, fast-shooting weapons no animal could outrun forever. How many times had this big dark deer lain motionless in a thicket while men like Rod crashed by on either side? Rod . . . barely a man without his rifle. . . . How many times had it been trapped, surrounded by a gang of hunters and forced to crawl back between drivers on its knees or, if discovered, forced into a low driving flight for its life, bullets screaming through the air around it? The fear! Perhaps it had even been hit, forced to spend a long cold winter nursing a painful wound while it foraged off sapling bark and twigs and acorns hidden under the snow. All those years fighting to survive, Norm thought . . . a losing battle against inferior beings.

He lowered his head to his arms, his cheek resting on the rifle stock, looked at the bright green of the crushed moss under his cheek, then up again at the magnificent creature, sighted, his finger on the trigger.

It would be an honor to share in its fate. . . .

*   *   *

"Let's go." Butch broke the silence at their end of the bar. He stóod up in the smoky gloom and drank off the last of his beer.

"Coming in for the big venison feed tonight?" Swede called as they got up.

They hesitated. "Ah, yeah. If it doesn't snow too much," Butch said. "The radio says there's a blizzard on the way. Otherwise we'll be in."

"Bring your drinking hats," Swede said. "The first quarter barrel's on me. And watch yourself out there now."

"Yeah, sure thing," Merald satd, and wiped the sweat on his forehead and followed the others outside, blinking in the brilliant sunlight. No inkling of snowfall in sight. Butch stuffed a large chew of snuff under his upper lip, then casually moved his bulk toward the jeep, the others drawn silently along, like mourners in a funeral procession, watching each other . . . being watched. . . .

They heaved themselves into the two jeeps and drove in silence toward the shack, going a few miles down the icy town road and turning off onto a gravel road for several miles. Just as they reached the narrow, rolling logging road that snaked three miles through the trees to the shack, they spotted a police car pulling out of their road.

"Sit tight," Butch said, and continued at speed past the police car and their turn-off. "He was down to our shack. We shoulda locked the gate." The others said nothing.

As soon as the police car turned a corner out of sight, Butch wheeled the jeep around and motioned for Rod, trailing him, to do the same and follow him down the road to the shack.

The jeeps swayed back and forth on the narrow rutted road, branches of trees scraping at their sides. Farther and farther they pulled into the woods, the silence between them deepening.

The day was still bright, and although a few scattered clouds raced ahead of the predicted blizzard, the snow still sparkled under the beat of the sun. They rolled down the windows to take in the exhilarating fresh air, pretending to peer into the forest to spot any white-tailed deer that lay snug in their beds. It was a good day to be alive—but none of them really noticed.

CHAPTER XV

After their near run-in with the police car, they followed Butch's instructions to stay away from the shack and scattered into the white magnificence of the forest, tiny figures in orange moving out along the high pine ridge and the hardwood flat between the ridge and the seven-mile swamp. Indications were that Norm hadn't been back to the shack.

Glenn eased off by himself, curiosity drawing him along the same track Norm had trod earlier that morning. Occasionally he felt the copy of the newspaper he'd stuffed into his shirt, knowing it was probably a bad idea to have taken it in the first place, except maybe not, it might be considered a natural thing for one of them to take it, why not him? . . . He tried to remember the look on their faces . . . was it suspicions of him . . . ? Or of each other, including him . . . ? And trying to absorb, and at the same time deny, that it might be one of them . . . ?

He paused, catching himself, bringing himself back here to the present, to the forest again, coldly squinting against the glare to survey the familiar terrain. To his left, the high pine ridge towered; hazel brush and the gray-green trunks of poplars thickened as they swept up the hill. Ahead, on the gently rolling flat, more thickets of hazel brush, scrub poplar and scattered clumps of green spruce filled in to provide good concealment in several directions. And to his right the entanglements of the seven-mile swamp—tag alder and marsh grass, scrub balsam and hemlock—presented a wall as thick as a tropical jungle. He'd seen it all before. And yet, without being aware of it, he had crouched slightly, brought his rifle across his chest and begun to pass his eyes knowingly over the thickets, probing for a first glimpse of Norm.

He stepped forward, moving with well-controlled tension, working well to the left of Norm's track, staying high, partway up the ridge, the high ground his, the initiative his. He sensed that Norm, in his stand-back, observant way, knew what was happening; but as always, Norm wouldn't know exactly how to respond, what to do.

A hundred yards along the ridge Norm's tracks abruptly turned and cut directly down into the thickets of the seven-mile swamp. Directly into the swamp—and they didn't come out. . . .

Unconsciously he sidestepped into the lee of a tree to look into the thickness of the swamp, considering what Norm could possibly be doing out there. To hunt out there was almost impossible. There were big bucks, but it was too thick and too noisy for one man to stand a chance. The difficulty of moving would sap a man in an hour. Norm had been gone six. Besides, one man couldn't hope to drag a buck out of that tangle. What could Norm be up to?

Unless . . . He crouched. Did Norm want him to follow? Did he want them both out there in the wet where no one ever went? Where a body could rot forever?

He backed in against the tree, the tangy pine scent in his nostrils. He peered out between the green needles, breathing with effort. To his front the

reaching fingers of the seven-mile swamp loomed
silently, a vast wilderness. He edged away, moving backward so as to keep facing toward the
swamp. . . .

A dim awareness of the night before homed in.
The two girls. He closed his eyes. What the hell had
he done? . . . The sounds and smells flooded his
mind: bodies by the dim lights of the dashboard,
watchful bodies, eyes gleaming, breasts thrust out, soft
magnets drawing his hand out against his will. "Hey,"
the indignant complaint from Sally, the chunky one
with the big tits under her sweater. He withdrew, his
grin sickly. But seconds later his look slid sideways;
those curves he could not avoid, a wonderful softness
that somehow drew him to swell higher and higher
. . . he reached again.

"Hey, goddamnit, the party's over. We're tired.
Let's just get back to town, all right?"

Bold little bitch. Magically the hunting knife appeared in his hand. The power in that blade was as
great as the blast from his rifle. And the fool girl
didn't even know.

"Hey!" She pushed him away, eyes wide now, the
note of uncertainty bringing her tone to the edge of
fear. He pulled back and she sat back, quietly, tensed,
her breasts moving up and down in rapid rhythm
beneath her sweater. He stared, the feel of the knife
still burning his hand, the bursting in his crotch more
than he could bear.

It got entangled after that. They were stopped in
the dark jeep, fearful voices in the dark. . . .
"Now," someone demanded . . . "now," the same
desperate voice . . . "*now* . . ." And the hard
nakedness of himself emerged into the cold. Reluctantly her slacks came off, the tall skinny girl frozen
in the back seat. He could take her next. He giggled,
spurting the instant his nakedness touched
her. . . . "All that hassle for *that*," Sally said, her

confidence returned. She tried to squirm out from underneath. "Why bother?" . . . He cursed her, refusing to move. Something inside him seemed to swell, a pressure he could not define, a movement of life they'd denied him all his life, Glenn Sr., Barbara. . . . His hands slid up over the smoothness of her breasts, upward as she struggled to get out from under him, his hands sliding on skin until her neck lay cradled within the power of his hands. . . . "Patty!" she choked.

The skinny girl jerked as if she'd been slapped. "Hey, stop!" she shrieked in a voice out of control. "Stop that. Please, stop that." In spite of her panic she thrust herself forward from the back seat, clawing at his shoulder in the dark, trying to pull his weight off Sally.

They'd turn him in, he'd thought, and the handle of his knife materialized in his hand again as the skinny girl tore at his head and back. He all but swung around, slashing the knife across her thin vulnerable neck, ripping away at the girl who'd taught young David how to fuck . . . but he managed control. The others knew he'd taken the girls back to town. The link would be there, the bloodstains in the jeep, the bodies, all of it hard evidence. . . .

He got up and put his hand on the skinny girl's throat, shoving her and her shrieks down into the back seat.

"Keep quiet," he said mildly, a request to a patient overly excited. He moved over and started the engine, ignoring Sally as she pulled herself upright and straightened her clothes. They drove on into town, the three of them silent, Sally huddled over against the door. On a deserted street at the edge of town he pulled over, opened his wallet and threw down a couple of twenties. "That's for your trouble. I'm sorry." Voice soft, apologetic.

Sally stared across the dim, green glow from the

dash lights, her eyes wet. She reached to pick up the bills, opened the door and stepped into a snowbank, Patty with her. She leaned back toward him. "You poor, sad sonofabitch," she said.

"Get out!" Glenn screamed in a voice he'd never heard, his hand going for the knife again. But the door slammed and the two girls clambered over the snowbank to the sidewalk. He jumped out on the driver's side, the cold air hitting him, an un-Glenn scream stilled at his lips, the pistol pulled from his belt. He stopped and watched the two girls walk away, glancing over their shoulders as they scurried along the icy sidewalk, a short plump girl and a tall skinny one, just a couple of working girls out to make a few extra bucks. He shrugged, turned and got back into the car. . . .

He gazed now at the cold, impersonal forest, at poplars stretching outward as far as the eye could see, a middle-class tree for making pulp for paper, not big, not significant, in truth all but unnoticed, each one lost because its kind dominated. A single tree was nothing—it lived and it died and no one noticed. He stared at a fallen poplar that was rotting and sinking into the earth. It lived and died, and no one noticed. It didn't *matter*. If he hadn't stopped here no one would even have seen it.

Again he touched at the newspaper inside his shirt, a deep sadness from the knowledge that he could not afford to do any more. . . .

He turned and began plodding up the face of the ridge, away from the jungle of the swamp. He saw through Norm's attempts to draw him out. If he did nothing, Norm could do nothing. It was the big man's way—the big man's failure. "Sorry, Norm," he said aloud. "You lose again. You just don't think right."

Then, far down the hillside to his right, he spotted

a hunched-over figure in red hunting clothes. Quickly
he slipped in behind a tree, raised his rifle and eased
it out around the trunk, annoyed over the lack of a
rest aim. The crosshairs came into focus, the check-
ered hunting clothes beyond. He almost laughed
aloud at what Norm was doing. His finger edged nervously at the trigger. The newspaper was forgotten.
How could he pass *this* up.

Abruptly he saw the rack lying near Norm, a creature as big as any deer he'd ever imagined existed,
killed by Norm alone in the depths of the swamp and
then dragged out alone.

Impossible. He spun in circles behind the pine tree,
two, three times, falling on his hands and knees in
the snow until his mind cleared. Carefully he brushed
the snow off his rifle, using a dry handkerchief to
clean the scope lens. "Easy now," he told himself in a
voice as calm as a windless day. He raised the rifle
again. Norm Petrie, the great hunter—with his guard
completely down.

CHAPTER XVI

Norm stood hunched over, dry spittle at the corners of his mouth, his sopping wet clothes covered with dirt and torn at the elbows and knees to expose skin bloodied from his long crawl. His dark eyes were glazed, hardly able to see the huge carcass at his feet. The big black, wrestled from the swamp, a giant of an animal, a trophy. He imagined entering the shack and throwing the big carcass at the others' feet . . . especially Rod's.

He started to drift sideways and put his hand on the trunk of a poplar to remain upright, the rubbery muscles of his aging legs straining to keep him on his feet, the process of dying working at his flesh. His head dropped to his chest, the face rugged, the lines deep, the black stubble of whiskers turning gray at the ends. Only the dark brown eyes were alert when he forced them to look.

The big black lay before him, a noble thing—and he had gunned it down.

In his mind the others gathered at his shoulders, pushing in against him with their unwashed bodies and breath sour with alcohol and cigarettes, sneering, cursing, ridiculing him. . . . The image of him-

self lay at his feet . . . a middle-aged man, a meat
hunter, the face sagging, the cooling flesh without
substance, without life. How could it compare with
what he'd brought down . . . ? Better go to the bars
and drink, call Joannie . . . feel the soft body of
the young girl, Sally, pushing up against him, her
hand reaching inside his pants, her hand plucking
twenties from his wallet, her hand opening the top of
his pants—

"*No.*" His body sagged tighter against the
tree. . . . And the one he wanted came to him.
His wife. Naked. Her eyes large, brown, direct, invit-
ing him to her, her first love. There could be no inhi-
bitions. No reason. She hovered in front of him, her
fingertips gentle on his face, his neck, his back, the
tight muscles of his stomach. Her lips touched his
cheek, then his lips, firm, soft, drawing him to her
and inside her, his hands working at the warmth of
her back. He lay back, she straddled his body, her
firm breasts enlarged, hanging toward his lips. He
pulled her close, kissing her nipples, caressing her
hips and back, pushing her away and touching the
firmness of her stomach, rubbing the lovely softness of
her pussy—He was up, ready to explode, his scrotum
firm and tight in the cold air. His hand moved down,
faster, faster, the image of her round firm breasts, her
flat stomach, the soft tangled hair of her pussy—the
body beautiful that he was no longer allowed to
touch, his own wife.

He winced, flinging the seed of himself into the
white of the snow, hunching forward.

Kablam.

Tugged by the vicious pull of an invisible hook, he
was spun to his right and toppled into the snow. The
sound of the shot pealed through his head, a painful
echoing noise that ruled the world. As though pulled
by a chain, he rolled sideways to press his cheek
tightly against the alligator bark of a large Norway

pine. In the split second he could have been nothing. Nothing.

The space of his move, and confusion, lasted only a few moments, in slow motion with his life in the center. The echoing crash of the rifle rang less loud and gave way to a deep burning in his right biceps. Norm, the great hunter, shot as he blew his seed into the snow. He grimaced, pressing his head tight against the tree.

Dismissing his exhaustion and the throbbing in his arm, he lifted his head up enough to look through the limbs of the balsams on the steep slope above. Whoever the man was, he had been too smart to take his track in the valley. Now he had the high ground, and once Norm dared to leave the covering shelter of pines he'd be badly exposed. He sank back in the snow. All along the ridge he could see nothing, but he knew better.

Trapped. He was aware of the deep throb in his arm now, aware too that he'd been successful in drawing the killer out—and trapping himself in the process.

What he needed was less rueful thinking and something to pinpoint the man's location. He pulled his rifle toward him, released the safety, crouched, tensed, and ran sideways through deep snow, shuffling quickly across a small opening where for a moment he was visible to anyone on the ridge. Nothing happened, and he sank down behind a pine tree, watching his flanks and down the ridge for signs that the man might be trying to circle him. He was acutely aware of the burning sensation in his arm, of his exhaustion. "Once more," he ordered himself, and again made his dash across the tiny clearing.

Still no response. He decided to patch up his arm. Wedging himself in as best he could behind an uphill balsam, with another on either flank, he took off his outer layers of clothes down to his white thermal un-

derwear. What had appeared to be simply a hole in
his woolen jacket turned out to be a mass of shiny
blood covering most of his left arm. "Only flesh," he
muttered as he stared at the oily-looking blood.

Using his hunting knife, grimacing, he cut a long
strip from the bottom of his thermal undershirt and
bound the wound tightly to cut off the bleeding, then
dressed, all the while checking the valley, his flanks
and the ridge. He would wait for nightfall to move,
the man should be gone by then, but once more
mixed in with the others, waiting. And next time he
might not miss.

Norm gazed through the trees at the huge carcass
of the big black, an unbelievable trophy, one he'd
needed in spite of himself. He winced, closing his eyes
against the fact of it, and against the realization that
at the critical moment he'd been lax.

He stood up, trying to put the past behind him.
His only chance was now, while he had a track, while
he had something to go on. Gripping his rifle, he
trotted through the deep snow across the small clearing. Nothing. Did the man know enough to wait until he had a still target? Or had he already taken off?

He peered up the steep slope, really more a small
mountain. Hazel brush and large poplars, not to men-
tion the deep drifts of snow between, made this an
impossible place for anyone to run. He swallowed,
spat, then stepped from behind the covering balsams.

Lifting his feet high to get through the snow, he
trekked uphill, rifle cleared for action, brown eyes
alert, probing the ridgeline as he made his painful
way, remembering the slope of the hill in Korea
where he'd known the machine guns waited, where
he'd known more of them would die.

He was worn out after wrestling so long with the
big black. His uphill progress slowed to a shuffle. He
grunted at each step, his skin prickling at the sense of
exposure whenever he crossed an open area. With

an old buck the muscles eventually grew stiff, he thought, the spirit to mate and to fight blunted by a body no longer matched for the task. Like an old Indian medicine man banished from the tribe, the buck wandered the hidden trails of the forest, wise in all the secrets of nature, a wisdom without usefulness because he could no longer act or lead. All that remained were memories and time—precious, disappearing time. Someday it would happen: a blizzard, starvation, coyotes, a chance bullet. There was no glory in death, only the fact of it—that and the end of time. You too, Norm.

He pressed on, the crest drawing slowly nearer until the ground suddenly leveled out and he stepped into the dark, soothing presence of the towering Norway pines on the ridge. Almost immediately he found the tracks and sank to his knees to catch his breath and to study the trail.

The snow was soft and granular, deep enough that it poured back in on itself the moment it was disturbed. These were fresh tracks all right, and moving fast. But just like the other day, he could not read the boot-markings. He glanced in the direction the tracks seemed to head. "Now, damn it, now."

He touched at the tender wound on his arm and noticed that the sky had clouded over. As sooon as he regained his wind, he picked up and started out following the tracks. Twenty feet along he froze. The track was a set-up, a trap. A simple fishhook move and the man would be able to see him coming and drop him cold. A wise old buck watched his backtrail. No. He'd have to parallel, skip in and out in a snake movement to be certain he stayed with the trail, a long, slow process, but the only way, like what he'd gone through to get the big black he'd left on the hillside.

Moving slowly, his legs like lead after struggling out of the swamp with the big black, he worked the ridge in long loops back toward the shack, several times swinging back to pick up the trail, stopping repeatedly to check out a particularly suspicious-looking clump of brush or trees where the man could easily lie in wait. He kept imagining that he'd make up for his earlier stupidity with experience and caution. He felt on fire, an intense involvement in the hunt such as he'd never imagined possible. Barbaric, but undeniably there.

After two painful, tiring hours in his stalk, he swung back to pick up the trail and found that it led at an oblique angle down the hill—a fishhook down and then back up again to take the high ground, he figured. He remained on the ridge, searching below and ahead along the ridgelines as the first flakes of snow started falling. After several minutes he spotted a figure in orange far down on the side of the ridge, moving slowly back toward the shack.

The line of his jaw hardened, the fire turned to cold fury. A killer out to bushwhack him, to kill him for no reason other, so far as he knew, except the pleasure of the kill.

He gripped his rifle, lifting his arms slightly to test his freedom of action, ignoring the sharp bite of pain at the back of his left biceps. "Now we'll see," he muttered, and started down the ridge, gravity with him now, moving to always keep trees and brush between him and *his* quarry. He was closing the gap, still unable to see the man clearly but sensing from what he could make out that he was kind of small . . . Rod or Glenn or—but he had no time for vague speculation now. . . . He crouched, easily staying with the man, moving from tree to tree in case the man turned, watching the orange coat and moving in unison. A few more moments he would have him clearly in sight—

"What the hell do you think you're doing, Petrie?" The voice boomed from the top of the ridge.

Norm whirled to see five of them standing partway up the ridge, staring down at him. The man in front of him turned and he saw it was the boy, David.

The others started down the hill, single file, a parade of orange—Merald, Butch, Bernie, Rod and Glenn. At some point when he'd circled out, the tracks must have met with the others, gotten mixed. . . .

"What the hell were you doing?" Merald demanded as they approached. He was short of wind. "What were you sneaking along after David like that for? You playing some damned stupid kind of game?"

Norm looked from one face to another, turning his body to control his wound. Don't tell them now, he thought through the crush of exhaustion and confusion. Not now. The killer must have seen him fall—so let him wonder what happened, let him stew, the pressure build, maybe he'd panic. . . . "Where's everyone been all day?" he managed to get out, hearing how hollow it sounded.

"Hunting," Butch said. "That's what we came for, remember? What the hell did you think?"

". . . Anyone get anything?"

"I had a shot earlier," Glenn said in a soft voice. "It was running through the brush, about a six-pointer. Down along the ridge past that big Norway pine that was struck by lightning."

Norm stared, looking from one to the other, the throbbing in his arm, in his legs, in the back of his head vicious.

"What the hell's with you, Norm?" Rod laughed, eyeing Norm's wet, torn clothes, the dirt covering them and his face, the curled, twisted mass of black hair filled with tiny icicles. "You look like you've been swamp-crawling again."

"Hey, you bleeding?" Bernie said, pointing.

Norm glanced at his bloodied shooting hand, from which he'd removed the mitten.

"You shoot something?" Butch asked.

"Yeah," Norm heard himself say as if from a distance. "I shot the big black."

"The big black?"

Norm nodded. "Out in the swamp by that island where I saw him once last year."

"You're a lying son of a bitch," Rod said. "I shot the big black and you know it. I don't see any fucking deer. I suppose you left it out in the swamp."

"It's back along the side of the ridge," Norm mumbled, fighting to keep his feet, fighting to focus on the swirl of the world around. "Just past the third saddle. He's there."

They stared as Norm slowly walked away with his rifle. The big black, he'd said, and somehow they believed him. "*I* got the fucking big black," Rod said without conviction. Heavy snow was beginning to fall and a strong wind buffeted up the hillside, a storm in the making. But they did not notice. They were taken by Norm's composure. Even now, on the verge of collapsing, the big man seemed to move through the snow and trees with a kind of grace, a naturalness that diminished them all.

"You and I are going to have to talk," Butch yelled, his tone an abrupt intrusion. "You and me, Norm. We'll talk. You hear?" Rod started to echo him, then for once shut his mouth.

Norm did not turn. Slowly, he continued away, his movements ponderous, a man in wet and bloodied rags on the verge of collapsing.

CHAPTER XVII

Norm woke up in a fog. It was night, he thought. He could not move. He hurt in every part of his body. . . . He sank back into a deep sleep. Weights were dragging at his mind. . . .

He opened his eyes in the black of the room, glancing out the uncurtained window beyond which he could barely make out the dark trunks of naked poplars swaying back and forth in the push of a steady northwest wind. Even inside the cabin he could sense the dropping barometric pressure, the thickening moisture, all the right signs for a major snowstorm in the making.

Somehow, while the others had gone back for the big black, he'd managed to stagger back to the dark-walled cabin with its rafters cluttered with antlers, the rock fireplace, woodpile, scattered bottles of booze, old furniture and the litter of boots and clothes. He had uncoiled slowly from the hunch he'd been in for hours and made his way to the bathroom, where he'd cleaned his wounds and bandaged them with thick white gauze soaked in Mercurochrome. Meticulously he'd purged the room of all traces of blood and burned his bloodied thermal underwear in

the fireplace, then stumbled into the back bunkroom
and collapsed. . . .

What was that—two, three hours ago in the gray
light of late afternoon? He couldn't say. He rolled
sideways and swung his feet to the throw rug beside
the bed. He grimaced with the agony of frozen, over-
worked muscles. He sat forward on the edge of the
bed, elbows on knees, staring at the floor as he fought
the dizziness brought on by the pain. He considered
falling back down on the bed but couldn't face the
agony of moving even that much.

Voices carried from the outer room, and he managed to get to his feet. He seized the side of the top
bunk for support and snapped on the naked light
bulb hanging from the ceiling.

Except for his baggy undershorts he stood naked,
scabs on his elbows and knees, a purple welt made by
the drag rope covering half of his right shoulder, the
bandage with its black splotch of dried blood on his
right biceps, the rest of his skin white and dry. When
he'd first met Joannie he'd still been solid, as firm as
in his high school football days when he was an all-
conference end . . . Now he was just sagging at the
old seams. . . .

He sucked in his stomach, recalling long-past times
lying in bed, Joannie feeling the firmness of his body,
a firmness he'd somehow have to find again. He swallowed, his teeth clenched. The law of nature, youth
challenging age. Stay strong, and smart, or die. It was
the law. The buck had found out. Now it was happening to him.

Aware now of the voices from the outer room, he
pulled on a set of dry thermal underwear to hide his
wound, shrinking away from the image of himself at
the moment he'd been shot, a humiliation that had
left him numb. "Oh, Jesus, Norman," he muttered
half aloud, "stop it. Stop it." He shook his head back
and forth.

*   *   *

"Well, I'll be damned—it lives," Rod said in a tight voice. He leaned against the bedroom doorjamb with a beer in his hand.

Norm only nodded, unwilling to trust his voice.

Rod stared at him, then away, his eyes making a circuit between the floor and the window. "It's snowing and blowing like hell out."

Norm nodded again.

"That's a nice buck you got there," Rod said in a casual voice. "We dragged it back and hung it up. I admit, it's a good one." He glanced back over his shoulder to see where the others were. He lowered his voice. "You know, you and I have the two biggest bucks ever taken out of this shack. This shack . . . for that matter, no other shack around here . . . has ever seen a year like this. Hell, Norm, I'd say you and I rate out pretty even, wouldn't ya say? I mean, we each shot a record buck. How you do it doesn't matter. Just as long as you bring it in, right?"

Norm stared. Rod, a little guy with a handsome face and greasy short-cut blond hair on his forehead, a tough little guy. "Yeah, right," he said.

Rod flared, his voice kept low so the others wouldn't hear. "You're on the edge, Norm. This whole fucking season you've been on the rag. You think you've got the world down pat. Well if you knew half the things going on in this world, it would change your damned high-and-mighty attitude in one hell of a hurry."

He thought he knew how to placate Rod, but he was damned if he felt like it. "Well, I'll tell you, Rod," he said in a drawl, more drawn out than he'd intended, "you tell me a piece of your hot information and I'll lay you eight to five it's not only bad news but old news. . . ."

Rod smiled. "That right, Norm? Well, old Norm . . . Norm, old buddy. . . . Try this one on for size. . . . My wife knows, and I know, and hell, I'd say just about *everyone* knows. Except you, that is." He hesitated, contemplating his leap into the gorge. He hadn't quite figured it to come out like this.

Norm looked at him. "I'm waiting, Rod."

"All right, since you asked, it just so happens that half the time Joannie's supposed to be working nights at the store . . . she isn't." Under the direct brown eyes that did not leave him for an instant, Rod's smirk faded. He straightened, fidgeting. "Shit, I'm sorry, Norm. I just thought you ought to know," he said, and turned away.

Norm stood there. A buzzing at the top of his head. Rod, angry little Rod, he'd say anything to get even . . . anything. But now there was a tightness in his chest that would not go away, seemed to be stopping his breathing. He felt a panic, he had to move, escape. He took a small, tentative breath, risked shrugging his shoulders, swiveling his neck and head, felt a pain go through him that he could almost relish—

"You and I are going to have a talk," Butch said as Norm carefully made his way into the kitchen.

Norm nodded, continued to the refrigerator, where he poured himself a glass of orange juice.

"We went into Swede's this morning," Butch continued, a wad of tobacco bulging in his left cheek. "They found that body, the one you said you saw yesterday by the old dynamite shack."

Norm drank his juice.

"Well?"

Norm shrugged.

"Well, damn it, that puts us all in a bind. We should have reported it. If the law finds out we discovered that body and didn't report it they're going to give us a lot of trouble. Failure to report something like that is a felony."

"Bad news," Merald said over Butch's shoulder. "God*damn* bad."

"I'll handle this," Butch snapped.

Merald backed away, face reddening.

"So we decided that if the law asks, which they probably will, we don't know anything," Butch said. "Understood?"

Norm shrugged. "Makes no difference to me. Something like this we can handle ourselves."

"There's nothing to handle," Butch yelled. "All you have to do is keep your mouth shut. Clear?"

"It's clear, but it doesn't solve anything."

"And you think one of us is involved, right?" Bernie asked in a reedy voice. "You think one of us shot him, don't you?" The others were stunned that the dumpy little man with the mixed drink in his bony hand, and Norm's friend, had been the first to put it out in the open like that. They sat waiting for Norm's answer, their opposition to the unthinkable so deep-seated that it became hypnotic. But Norm could smell the fear. What's going on? they screamed silently.

"Well say so, goddamnit," Butch said, grabbing the front of Norm's underwear.

"I just *found* the body," Norm said in his calm voice. "Someone else shot him, and the two others."

They stood in a circle between the living area and the kitchen counter, each of them with a drink in hand, center stage, isolated from a world that no longer existed. They only existed here, deep in the forest, enclosed by the walls of this shack, part of its fixtures, like the white gas stove and refrigerator, the round kitchen table, the cold gray floor and the old maroon rug, the heavy split-log easy chair, the old sofa with the sagging springs, the pieces of bark on the cement floor by the wood box, the piles of thick hunting clothes, the rack of powerful rifles. Wind buf-

feted the shack, the blizzard working itself up to full
force.

"Look at you guys," Butch said. "You act like you
believe Norm."

"I don't believe shit," Rod said.

"Ever since Saturday when Norm came back here
with that cock and bull story about someone pointing
a rifle at him, and him swimming under the goddamn
ice, everyone has been walking around like they have
a corn cob up their ass. Makes me sick. That story
somebody maybe shot at him. And he found that guy
who was shot. That's it. And now you all act like the
world's coming to an end. Well, look around you,
damn it. You know each other. You know how long
we've been together. Take a look. Can any of you hon-
estly say you believe what Norm's saying?"

They shook their heads. Butch, the leader, talked
sense.

"Tell us, Norm," Butch went on, "with what you
have to go on, do you *really* think it's possible?"

Norm stared across the kitchen counter, imagining
himself in an old western movie. Joannie, dressed in
ruffles and black net stockings, glanced casually to
watch him handle this. His juices began to flow.

"You're still ignoring the girl that was killed last
year where we were hunting. And the other guy three
years ago."

"Three years ago!" Butch said. "What do you want,
Norm? A dozen guys a year get killed during the season in this state. So a couple got killed up here. And
they might have been in an area we hunted in. But
you don't even know that for certain. You don't even
know if we were in there the same day they were
shot."

"We were in there," Norm said. "Like it or not, we
were in there, both times."

"Oh, you bastard," Merald said with sudden vehemence. His face closed up, the thick cheeks puffed, the heavy lips curled. "Where do you get the right to make accusations like that?"

Norm shrugged.

Butch, his leathery face bright red, his fists clenched, started to speak, but Glenn spoke up. "This is crazy to be talking like this. We're supposed to be civilized human beings. If something's wrong, let's for god's sake report it to the law like we're supposed to. They're paid to handle things like this."

"All right with you, Norm?" Merald said.

"Sure," Norm said. "The evidence is circumstantial but—"

"Then why the accusations?" Glenn said.

"Because there are three dead people."

"You better go visit a shrink," Rod said. "Wasn't that eighteen-pointer enough? You still have to make up stories?"

"I'm sick and tired of this crap," Butch said, pushing his stubby forefinger at Norm. "Understand? It's ruining everything. And I say it's all made-up crap."

"There's still three dead people—"

"No!" Butch smashed his fist against the kitchen counter, cracking the top. "I said, no more. I don't want to hear it." He went around the counter and grabbed hold of the front of Norm's red woolen shirt. "Damn you, Norm . . . you're fucking everything up—"

Norm drove his hands up between Butch's arms, snapping them outward and breaking his grip, and Butch, with surprising swiftness, retaliated, swinging a meaty fist, landing it flush on Norm's cheek, the thwack of bone on flesh like a rifle shot inside the confines of the shack. Norm staggered backward, against the refrigerator, shaking his head and raising his long arms to fend off Butch, who now moved in to follow up his advantage. Three, four times Butch swung, haymakers that landed on arms, shoulders and the back of Norm's lowered head.

The two big men struggled, their forms and movements filling the kitchen, the shouts of the others barely coming through to them. . . . "Stop it, you'll wreck the place . . . way to go, Butch . . . old Norm's had it. . . ."

Norm kept the refrigerator at his back, stayed in a tight crouch trying to block Butch's fists, watching until Butch paused for a breath. Then, launching himself off the refrigerator and onto his toes, Norm snapped his large frame forward, concentrating all his weight behind his fist, the force of his blow jolting all the way up to his shoulder, ripping at his wound. Butch staggered backward, catching onto a chair and crashing to the floor in the living room.

Norm did not follow. "I've had enough," he said, as Butch got back to his feet. They glared at each other, the others milling in between. Butch managed a laugh. "You bastard, Petrie, that was a pretty good shot. I wonder if you have anymore. Someday we'll have to find out." He shrugged Merald off his arm.

"Hey, look at the blood!" Glenn seemed especially animated for him, pointing at the mass of red on Norm's left arm where his wound had been wrenched open. "What happened, Norm?"

For several moments Norm did not answer, searching around the room, working it over in his mind. He couldn't hold back anymore now . . . the game was out of the bag. . . . He turned to Glenn. "It's a bullet hole."

"A *what?*" Butch yelled. "What kind of crap—?"

"It happened just after I dragged the big black out of the swamp. That's why I was following David. I was snaking on the trail of the guy who shot me and I must have accidentally picked up David's track—"

"Let me look at that." Butch came forward to help Norm peel off his wool shirt, then took a knife and cut off the sopping red sleeve of underwear and the thick gauze bandage.

"That's a bullet wound, all right," Glenn said as they all edged close to see the deep furrow that oozed a steady stream of blood.

"No." Merald's face sagged. "You know what that would mean. . . ."

Bernie laughed nervously.

"So it looks like a bullet hole," Rod said. "So what?"

"What do you think, Butch?" Merald asked weakly. He wiped at his rimless glasses.

"What am I supposed to think?" Butch snapped. "It *looks* like a fucking bullet hole. I don't know, why the hell should I do all the thinking?"

"From opening day I've been trying to tell you . . . it's there, the man's here . . . another man is dead. . . ."

Faces waiting for a reprieve that would not come, staring eyes fixed on Norm, eyes filled with outrage, hate, and fear. Finally Norm pulled away and started to move across the room.

"Where're you going?" Butch said.

"To bandage my arm." Norm glanced down where blood dripped from the tips of his fingers, making small puddles on the dirty linoleum of the kitchen floor.

"And then what?"

"That's up to you."

"What *are* we going to do, Butch?" Bernie asked.

"We should have gone to the authorities right off," Glenn said, almost primly, though the tone was lost on the others. His even-shaped face appeared tight, the mildness drained. "It was the only thing to do—"

"You said that *before*, goddamnit," Butch told him. "All right, all right, let's go to the damn cops."

Merald asked, "Can we make it through this snow? There must be six or eight inches already and it's blowing like hell. It'll be bad drifted and your four-wheel drive isn't working."

"I can drive through it," Rod said. "My four-wheel drive is fine. I'll go—"

"You ain't going anywhere," Butch said.

"Who says so?"

"Hey, fellas," Glenn said, feeling the sweat pouring from his armpits, "we've got enough trouble, let's not—"

"And why can't I go?" Rod asked, ignoring Glenn. "If you're trying to say something, Butch, just spit it out."

"If we go, we all go . . . if we stay, we all stay—"

"I'm not staying here," Merald said quickly. "No way. Glenn's right. We've got to get to the law. And now." His gaze took in the room, coming to rest on the gunrack where his three hunting rifles hung. Without thinking, he moved across the room toward them.

"Stay away from those guns," Butch yelled.

"They're mine . . . I just wanted to check them out. . . . I just wanted—" His voice was close to a whine, but fear was its dominant note. . . .

"Dad," David called out, but too late as Butch swung a hard open-palm blow to the side of Merald's head, knocking the big man to the floor. "Settle down, dammit." Butch stood spread-legged, breathing heavily, sweat glistening on his sunburned neck and jowls. "We'll go to town. All of us. Together."

"In this storm?" Bernie asked.

"In this storm," Butch said, ignoring Merald, who was still on the floor, looking in front of him, seeing nothing. "Bigmouth Rod said he could make it."

"Your fucking-A," Rod said.

A huge gust of wind buffeted the shack. Snow rattled off the windows and scraped along the old log walls that were creaking before the fury of the storm.

Involuntarily the hunters in the shack hunched their shoulders a little, looking silently up at the ceiling past the clutter of antlers.

They would not look at each other.

CHAPTER XVIII

A blurred sheet of white before the headlights, a moving wall blotting out all the world ten feet beyond the hood. The huge trunks of trees loomed and faded. Rod jerked the wheel on the four-wheel-drive jeep, threading them down the narrow logging road, cursing when the vehicle bucked into a drift and sent an avalanche of snow curling up over the hood, blinding them. Gears grinding, wheels spinning, somehow they broke through and pushed on, the blizzard driving at the window, hypnotizing, filling all their vision.

The jeep slewed sideways. Something smashed against the right side, a crunching of metal on wood. Rod jerked the transmission from low to reverse, trying to rock the jeep. It would not move.

"Ya son of a bitch, why didn't you stay on the road?" Butch slammed his hand down on the dashboard.

"I can't *see* the road."

"Well, I can't open my damn door. Let us out your side. We'll have to push."

One by one they struggled out of the jeep into the blizzard. The bitter wind burned their faces and necks, cut through their coats as if they stood naked. Hard snow stung their faces like buckshot, forcing their heads down.

"Over here. Put your shoulders to it," Butch yelled, his voice whipped away by the wind. "Rock it, Rod. Rock the sonofabitch."

Back and forth, back and forth, they stumbled and pushed and fell against each other, floundering in knee-deep snow beside the narrow logging trail, the jeep roaring, wind howling, snow slashing.

"If we don't get this bastard out of here we'll freeze to death," Merald said.

"Push," Butch yelled, and they gave it one more effort, muscles bulging, almost popping. But they could not break free.

"Let's push it away from this tree," Norm said, his deep bass voice barely audible in the storm. "It's binding up against the tree. I think that's what's stopping us."

"We're gonna freeze," Merald told him. "It was your stupid idea to try this—"

"It's only a mile or so back to the shack," Butch yelled. "We can walk it if we have to—"

"We'll get lost. We'll freeze. . . ."

"Goddamnit, get over here and push," Butch said, seizing the back of Merald's coat and manhandling him up against the side of the jeep.

"Push, goddamnit, push," Butch bellowed, his voice taking on a desperate edge. "Rock it, goddamnit, Rod. Rock the sonofabitch."

"Together they huddled at the back of the jeep, grunting, heaving, sweating as they floundered and grappled for footing. Miraculously it did move ahead, two, three feet, snow spinning out from all four wheels, the men running with the jeep, grunting, Merald falling to one side, Bernie sprawling on top of him. But they were free and back on the road.

Slowly they managed to crawl back inside the jeep

with Rod. Glenn and David sat on the floor behind
the back seat; Norm, Merald and Bernie crammed
themselves together on the rear seat, and Butch rode
jump seat. For the most part, other than Butch and
Rod snarling back and forth about Rod's driving,
they were silent, soaking in the steamy heat of the
jeep, barely visible to each other in the meager green
glow of the dash lights.

"Hey, watch it!"

The jeep slewed into a large drift and another
blanket of snow billowed across the windshield.
There was a spinning, floating sensation like the
timeless state between wakeful reality and a vivid
dream, an anxious space of weightlessness, then a brutal, twisting smack of flesh squishing against metal,
bones jarring each other.

They lay in pain and darkness, a mass of bodies in-
tertwined like a ball of snakes in a den. . . .
"Jesus, I'm hurt". . . . "What the hell happened?" . . . Movement, bodies writhing about for
the solid feel of reality. . . . "Y'fucker, Rod, ya
tipped us *over*—"

"Gas!" Merald's voice. "I smell gas!"

"Which way are we turned? . . . Gas! It's gonna
blow—"

"We're on the side." Norm's calm voice carried in
the blackness. "There's gas, all right. We better get
out . . . I think we're on a steep incline—"

"I got the door," Rod said.

"Get the hell off me."

Bernie's high cackle came from a place near the
bottom of the pile. Somehow in the mass of churning
bodies he'd managed to get his flask out of his coat
pocket and take a long drink.

The latch clicked and a swirl of icy wind and snow
drove into the cave of the jeep. "Oh God," Merald
wailed.

One by one they managed to stand and pull themselves out into the black of the storm—all except Merald, who lay at the bottom of the jeep. "My leg, it's my knee. I can't move. Help me. Christ, I smell gas. It's all over me."

"Dad," David yelled, and started to climb back inside.

"Hold it," Norm said, stopping the boy. "We'll get him out of there."

"I'll get the bastard," Butch growled, and crawled back inside the jeep, Glenn following along. The wind howled and snow rattled off the jeep, muffling the cursing and whimpers and grunts that came from inside. Eventually Merald's head emerged and Rod and Norm took hold of his shoulders. Butch and Glenn were below, shouldering Merald's broad rump, grunting and heaving as Merald wormed his huge midriff over the edge of the jeep's roof, then abruptly tumbled, face first, into the waist-deep drift on the steep incline beside the logging trail. "Oh God, my knee. . . ."

Floundering in the deep snow like wounded animals, they pulled the almost helpless two-hundred-and-sixty-pound man up toward the road, snow stinging at their faces, the wind cutting deep into their flesh. "We're gonna freeze." Merald was lost to panic now. "I knew it, I knew it. . . ."

In the dark of the swirling storm Bernie laughed, coughed, drank deeply from his sterling-silver flask and coughed some more.

"What should we do?" Glenn asked, his words, sounding frightened, all but lost in the storm.

They stood in a tight little circle with hands stuffed in their pockets and hats pulled low over their heads. Merald's body was a mound at their feet, David kneeling beside it. They were face to face and could scarcely see each other's outlines—and then only if they were not looking into the wind.

"It's more than a mile back to the shack," Butch said. "Another mile out to the gravel road and then seven or eight to the nearest place."

"If we stay here we'll freeze," Glenn said. "It must be close to ten degrees, with a wind chill twenty below or worse—"

"The jeep'll cut the wind," Rod yelled.

"Three or four hours and we'd still freeze to death," Glenn said. "We don't have the clothes to stay out here all night. And a fire'll blow the gas."

"But if we try for the shack we might get lost," Butch said.

"What about Merald?" Rod said. "Leave him, get your jeep and come back—?"

"Oh, no, please, don't leave me—"

"My four wheel drive isn't working," Butch said. "Remember? There's no way I could drive more than a few feet."

"Well, what about Merald?"

"Well, goddamnit, if you woulda stayed on the road we wouldn't be here."

"Ya think I did it on purpose? The snow had drifted out there, the road dropped away, I couldn't see. It damn sure wasn't on purpose—"

"I ain't so sure," Butch said.

"What the hell does that mean?" Rod knew damn well what that meant. . . . The SOB was accusing him of being the killer amongst them. . . . He'd better watch it or he'd kill the sonofabitch. . . .

"Settle down," Norm told them, realizing what was happening but having no time to relish it now. "For God's sake take a look around you. Get ahold of yourselves. We got to work together, get organized and try for the shack. It's damn cold out here, likely to get colder. We could be a couple days in that jeep. I don't know if we could hack the cold. If we make some kind of sled for Merald I think we can make the shack—"

"If we wander off the road we're dead," Glenn said, punctuated by another fit of giggles from Bernie.

"Gimme that damn flask." Butch yanked it from Bernie's hand. "You get drunk now and I'll be damned if we'll carry you."

"Hey—"

"Let's get going."

They dragged the removable bottom part of the back seat from the jeep and tied two pieces of hemp rope, kept in the jeep as a drag rope for deer, to the frame, turned the seat so the smooth vinyl side was against the snow and then helped Merald crawl up on the springs. "Two guys to a rope. We'll switch off," Norm said as they strained forward.

Twenty, thirty yards they bulled forward. Nowhere was the snow less than calf deep, and sometimes they floundered into deeper drifts, bumping against each other, fingers freezing as they struggled to keep a grip on the knotted rope. The snow blew into their faces and down the napes of their necks, collecting inside their coats and at the tops of their boots. Even with the wind following, the storm drove the cold directly into the marrow of their bones. They could not see and only scarcely feel the tracks the jeep had pushed into the snow, tracks that were already drifting over.

"No, damn it." Rod threw down his rope. "Merald's too goddamn heavy. We'll never make it."

They paused, sucking for air, sweating in their crotches and armpits, freezing everywhere else.

"What're you talking about," Merald called from his litter. "We can make it, we can make it—"

"I'll help, dad." David knelt beside his father.

"He's too damn heavy. I tell you we'll all freeze trying to drag him out," Rod said. "Let's put him in the jeep and we'll come back."

"No you won't . . . don't leave me, I know you won't come back. . . . Hey, *please*—"

"Then walk, goddamnit," Rod said.

"I can't, my damn knee—"

"We can make it," Norm called above the howl of the storm. "Rod, take a break. David, you pull. Let's go."

"Never make it," Rod muttered, and stepped off to the side as they struggled past, Glenn and Butch and Norm and David pulling at the two ropes.

Norm in the lead, they toiled in a howling, swirling world of black, an unseen carpet of snow dragging at their feet, anchors on the muscles of legs forced to pick up high for every step. Somehow they dimly recognized the open expanse of the road, sensing the swaying trees of the forest on either side, towering objects that rattled and crashed together. Step after step, a ponderous movement through a world in which no other human being existed. They had no past, no future, only the now and the black wind, the drifts clawing at their legs and the cold numbing their faces and freezing their hands into curled fists around the slippery icicles of the drag ropes.

Occasionally, like the slap of a prodigious rifle in the wind, something crashed. Twice they crossed large trees that must have fallen across the road minutes before, struggling up over these roadblocks, realizing what could have happened if they'd been passing in the jeep at the time. . . .

They paused and fell to their hands and knees in the deep snow, muscles exhausted, faces and fingers without feeling. They could not go on, but to stay was to die. Each pause was longer. And the cold worked deeper.

"Hey, what the—?" Butch said as they all bumped together, faced with a dark wall, a small clump of balsam, and to either side the swaying trunks of poplars. He went off a few feet to one side, the trees invisible when he faced into the wind, and only the dim impressions of black shadows when he looked downwind. Everywhere he turned there were trees two or three feet away. Even when he walked back behind the makeshift sled there were trees that they must have passed by inches with their heads down.

"We're *off* the road," Butch yelled as he circled, repeated it three, four times as he lumbered around them.

"Can't be." Rod set out to repeat Butch's circle, disappearing into the swirling black.

"Looks like it's all over," Bernie said, sobering fast.

"Maybe we can dig in by the trees here and weather it out," Glenn said, voice soft. He sounded close to tears, merely a gentle dentist about to freeze to death. Death. . . .

"What's going on?" Merald called out. "You guys aren't serious. . . . Norm, you're supposed to lead the way back—"

"Rod." It was Norm shouting into the night. "Rod." Nothing came back but the howling of the wind as it knifed its way through the forest, tree limbs fanning at the air, poplars swaying, branches clattering together, the nearly horizontal sweep of graining snow rattling off the trees and sliding along the ground snow, the cacophony deafening them.

It was age, Norm thought, or the revenge of the big black, or both, that had sapped him of his strength. Or his job, or Joannie, or the bullet the killer had put into his arm and the loss of blood and strength. . . . Whatever, he could now pull on the rope with only one arm, an arm that had stretched itself into a near-useless limb, the curled fingers frozen numb like his legs, like his mind as he struggled to make the next step. The next step . . . somewhere along the way he's failed to concentrate, to sense their way through the forest as he had at the start, to listen, to detect the dim path of white snaking through the huge black canyon of trees. Nature had taken over, and was winning.

He could sense no light, no opening. If they did not find the road they would die, a certainty. And the killer would die with them. Was that a comfort . . . ?

Recklessly, he released his grip, let his mind wander. . . . Joannie, right at this moment, would be gliding about the bright warmth of their house, maybe getting ready to go out to dinner, a chance to get out, and at dinner, around her shoulders and the bare nape of her slim neck, the warmth of the room would curl unnoticed. And afterward they— she!—would get into her car and drive to a warm place . . . drive home, damn it, alone . . . never mind what Rod had said about her. Alone . . . except he was the one who was alone . . . better face that. Alone. . . back there, and here. Nothing for it but to try to survive. . . .

A voice, without a scratch of pride. "Do *something*. Somebody do *something*." Merald the adult-infant, wounded, mewling from where he lay on the springs of the car seat.

"Hey, Norm, I thought you were watching," Butch said, but now his voice was without even the force of anger.

"What do we do?" Bernie's giddiness now wholly replaced by fear. No one heard him as he curled forward into the snow, his hands in his pockets. He lay still, waiting.

"I can find the road," Norm said, mostly to himself, for himself. "We'll be all right—"

"Where's Rod?" Glenn said, looking around, seeing nothing except big-deal Norm. Norm, who bore his mark, who belonged to him . . . sooner or later.

"Rod," Norm yelled into the wind. "I don't know,"

he said, "but we've got to go on. . . . Where's Bernie?"

"I don't know," Glenn said . . . Glenn and Norm . . . partners . . . made for each other . . . He would have smiled if the cold hadn't frozen his face. As it was he could barely call out, "Bernie . . ."

"What?" A gravel voice from off to the side. Slowly, helped by Norm, Bernie crawled to his feet.

"Grab the rope and we'll turn this around," Norm told them. They rolled Merald off into the snow, turned the makeshift sled around and took up their places—Butch, David, Glenn and Bernie pulling on the two ropes and Norm just ahead, feeling his way forward into the onslaught of the wind, sensing with his feet the hollow track the sled had made coming in.

A strange sound carried with the storm, a change in the wind? A whine, a whimper? Norm stopped, the others halting behind him. Sure enough, something off to the side. . . . He moved over to investigate. A dark object huddled in the snow. . . . "Oh God, no. Please, God, help me, please. . . ."

Rod.

"Rod?"

"Norm!" He said the name with relief, scrambled to his feet, instantly trying to recover, cover up. . . . "Where were you guys? I've been yelling like hell. Why didn't you answer me?"

"We didn't hear you. C'm'on," Norm said, putting an arm around Rod's—the killer's?—shoulders.

Rod jerked away. "Forget it. We lost the road, we don't have a chance—"

"Quit your damn whimpering and act like a man." It felt good to let something out. "I think I can find the road—"

"Who's whimpering? You watch your mouth. . . .

Okay, let's get going if you're so damn sure you can do it. . . ."

Less than fifty feet along he felt the opening to his left, a thin pathway of white—the road. He turned them to put the northeast wind on their right shoulder, the proper direction to the shack.

Now in the lead, struggling to keep a hold on his concentration, Norm was sure they could make the shack—except for Merald. Their clothes were caked with snow, their gloves sopping, beaded with ice.

"We've got to leave Merald," Rod whispered to Norm more than once. "He'll be the death of us all. . . ."

And finally they did leave Merald. There was no choice. Fifteen agonizing feet, and then collapse. Ten feet, and then collapse. Five, and collapse. That was it. They could not move him at all.

Norm knelt. "We'll put the seat over you to keep off the wind. We'll get Butch's jeep and be back—"

"Please don't leave me." Both Merald's hands were gripping Norm's coat. "A thousand bucks, ten thousand bucks . . . just as soon as we get back. Norm . . . please. . . ."

"Stay under the seat," Norm told him, feeling his concentration fade, the strength of his voice too. They had no choice. He pried Merald's hands from his coat and stood up.

"David, David," Merald pleaded to his son.

"We'll be back," Norm said, firmly turning David around. The boy was too exhausted to resist.

They left his father lying in the snow, staggered away, prisoners shackled in chains, Norm in the lead.

Merald started crawling after them.

Less than fifty yards, and Norm . . . his mind fuzzy, his head lowered to the slow drag of one foot in front of the other, his good arm around Bernie's waist . . . smacked into a solid object, a large piece of metal smooth to the touch. He rubbed both hands on

the metal, feeling it up and down, recognition taking
forever to sink in.

Butch's jeep. They'd made the shack.

And each of them had, as never before, shown himself to the others.

CHAPTER XIX

They had no electricity. A tree across the wires, they figured. But they had a kerosene lamp lit, and the fireplace roaring, and the oil burner blasting. They winced at the thousands of needles prickling at their frozen hands and ears and toes as circulation slowly returned. They were alive.

"You did a good job, Norm," Butch said in the midst of the camaraderie. He wrapped his meaty arm around Norm's shoulders. "I've got to admit, I was about ready to give it up out there. When we got off that road I figured we were finished—"

"Me too." Bernie laughed, a water glass full of whiskey in hand. His normally blue-white face was flushed with excitement, his eyes bright as he looked back and forth among them. "When you guys said the road had disappeared, well, it was like someone pulled the plug. I just fell in the snow. I think I was asleep when old Norm pulled me up. That would've been it, I didn't feel a thing."

"I figured Rod was a goner," Glenn said, his calm back in place. "When he made that circle and didn't answer I began to wonder—"

"No problem," Rod said, glancing at Norm. "I figured I'd find the road easy enough, but then I wasn't sure if I could find you guys again and lead you out."

"Even after we found the road it didn't look good," Glenn said chattily. "This is about as bad a blizzard as I've ever seen."

"Well, by God, hauling Merald like that on the jeep seat," Butch said, "that was pretty good thinking"—he couldn't quite bring himself to credit Norm by name—"but that thing really just plowed snow, and with two hundred and sixty pounds to boot. . . ."

Merald lay sprawled on the sofa, his swollen knee propped on some pillows, drink in hand, David sitting nearby. Merald's features were pulled tight. True, within minutes after leaving him they'd returned and carried him to the shack. But the point was, they'd abandoned him, left him out there to freeze, to die. His face showed how he felt.

"I don't know what you're pissed about," Butch said, reading the look. "We worked our asses off for you. Hauled you until we couldn't move. If the shack would have been more than a few hundred yards away I don't think we'd have made it. None of us. And it would have been on account of you."

Merald gave him a disgusted look, handed over his glass to David for a refill. David jumped quickly, small atonement for the guilt over leaving his father.

Butch flopped down into an easy chair in front of the roaring fireplace. He shook his head, contemplating the flames, rubbed at his hands, still feeling the burning sting of thawing out. "You don't face something like this every day," he said solemnly. "We faced a hell of a situation. And I think we did a helluva job." He thrust a meaty finger toward Merald. "We saved your goddamn life, Merald. Hauled your ass through all that snow. Damn near killed ourselves, and you're here all safe and sound."

Merald said nothing.

"Well, isn't that right?" Butch's face was turning red.

"Yeah, yeah, it's right." But Merald hadn't relented.

"Not many people can say they ever lived through a blizzard like that," Bernie said. "I hung with you guys. I couldn't pull at the end there, but I stayed up with you guys. . . ."

"You did all right, Bernie," Glenn said. "You were right in there—"

"If it wouldn't have been for Rod running the goddamn jeep off the road I think we would have made it," Butch said. "We were going all right."

"Dammit to hell, Butch, I couldn't see. That drift went three or four feet off the road. I couldn't tell the road dropped away. Hell, ya'd think I did it on purpose."

"Maybe you did," Butch said. For the second time.

And with the words their sense of shared adventure was killed. For a few brief moments the bond had been complete, solid, like the bond between soldiers who have shared the rigors and dangers of combat. Three brief words ended it.

Rod got to his feet, softened by the flickering red light of the fireplace and the soft glow of the single kerosene lamp. His voice was not soft. "What do ya mean by that?" Words delicate, intended to draw Butch to his feet.

Butch stayed where he was, not wanting to take it further . . . this thing they could not believe, could not handle, that tore at them all.

But Rod still saw only the challenge. "Well, what do ya mean, ya sonofabitch?"

"Call me that one more time, Rod, and you won't be calling anybody anything for a long time." But Butch kept his weary legs propped on the frayed footstool.

Glenn stood up, placed himself in front of the fireplace between them. "Listen, fellows, we just barely managed to escape with our lives. It might be days before we can get out of here. Somehow we're going to have to get along." He liked that image of himself, almost paternal, peacemaker . . . great hunter Norm wasn't the only one who could take charge . . . and it would keep them together longer, give *him* more time. . . .

"Ah!" Rod waved Butch away and sulked back to lean against the kitchen counter. "I just know one thing, *I* ain't going to sleep as long as our buddy Butch here is awake—"

Butch lurched forward, spilling half his drink. But as quickly as he stood he tumbled to the floor. "Got a damn charley horse," he groaned, rubbing at his huge leg.

"Well, isn't that—"

"Rod, keep your mouth shut," Norm said. "We've got enough trouble here." He eyed Rod more closely than he meant to. . . .

Rod waved him away, but he nonetheless remained back, leaning against the counter.

With Glenn's help, Butch managed to get back in his seat in the easy chair, wincing and rubbing at his thigh. "Rod, as soon—"

"Butch . . ." Norm said, "somehow we're going to have to get along until we can get out of here." And, he hoped, stay alive.

"Then keep him the hell away from me." Butch leaned back and settled in as Bernie brought him a fresh drink. . . .

The fire burned steadily, Norm or Glenn feeding it when necessary. The lamp burned on the kitchen counter, dimly illuminating the men sprawled around the fireplace. They sat with their eyes fixed on the flames, sometimes shifting sideways to risk a furtive glance at their shackmates. The blizzard continued to buffet the shack, a constant reminder of what they'd just escaped. Except for Norm, they were filled with a sense of their accomplishment, a struggle with death they'd survived.

But they were exhausted. They drank booze steadily, their minds going numb again, their thoughts wavering. Outside the log walls the storm raged. Half the night loomed ahead, and then tomorrow and the next night. . . .

Merald, sprawled on the sofa, began to snore, scowling even in his sleep. Bernie, stretched out in an easy chair, dropped his glass, his head lolling to one side. Butch opened his eyes at the thump of Bernie's glass on the tattered throw rug. He looked around the room, struggling to focus. "We're going to have to get some sleep," he muttered. The others nodded. No one moved.

"How's your arm, Norm?" Glenn asked quietly.

"Stiff, but not too bad."

"Norm," Butch said, "we can't keep this up." He had calmed down some. "Now, let's suppose that things have been happening like you say. You're going to have to help us, damn it . . . you must have some ideas about . . . who . . ."

The others were instantly as alert as their exhausted condition would allow—even Bernie, lifting his head, squinting as if trying to see where Butch's words were leading. Only Merald continued to snore.

He decided he'd tell them less and more, see what happened. . . . "I've never come close even to seeing the guy, although I think I might have some evidence the police can use in their lab to show who he is." Which was a lie. He watched them for a tell-tale hint, anything that might give him an advantage. Nothing.

"What's that?" Glenn asked, surprised that he'd allowed himself to speak up.

"I guess I won't say just yet—"

"And you don't have the foggiest damn idea either,

do ya?" Rod broke in. "I know one thing, though. Whenever Butch is awake, I'm going to be awake."

Butch sat forward. "One more word, Rod, and you're going to have a busted head—"

"How about everyone hitting the sack?" Norm said. "Everyone's wore out from the storm. I could keep watch for a few hours and then we can figure something else out."

"What the hell are you going to watch *for?*" Rod said, knowing the answer. "Or should I say who . . . ?" He looked at Butch.

The others just stared, their eyelids drooping, eyes dulled. They'd been through enough; they deserved a rest. Norm could be the lookout. Norm they could trust. After all, he'd been the one shot. . . .

One by one they struggled to their feet, even Merald, who used David like a crutch to hop into one of the back bunkrooms.

"If you get too sleepy, wake me up," Butch told Norm.

"And me too," Rod said quickly.

Bernie staggered sideways and stumbled over a footstool. Norm helped him up. He grinned, barely coherent. "A'm awright. Stayed with you guys out there. Yessir." His head bobbed. "An', an' tomorrow I'll help git us outta *here*. Yessir. . . ."

"You did fine, Bernie," Norm said, guiding him toward the back room. "You did a helluva job. Now get some sleep."

The others went to bed and passed out almost immediately, Norm figured by the volume of snoring. He shuffled about the room, going into the bathroom to check his wound with a flashlight, putting a pot of coffee on the gas stove, adding wood to the fire. He blew out the kerosene lamp to conserve fuel and settled down on the sofa to stare into the flames.

Finally he stood and walked slowly around the room, aware that his legs had no strength, that his

body verged on collapse. All morning long that crawl
through the swamp after the big black. And the worst
was that drag through that tangled tag alder swamp.
Just this morning, and it seemed like a week ago.
And then the shot, and the stalk, and the storm, and
the wallowing through the deep snow after the accident, and then manhandling Merald. . . .

Time ticked past. He sipped scalding black coffee
and fed the fire and stared into the flames. Outside
the storm showed no sign of relenting. Even if it
cleared they couldn't get out. Someone would have to
snowshoe out to the main road. His head bobbed between thoughts. All this time and he had not a clue.

Only that the man was here.

Maybe he could at least narrow it down . . . to
Rod? Butch? The figure out there had seemed smaller
. . . maybe Glenn . . . ? Unlikely, damn unlikely. Besides, it was young David he'd seen, mistook
for the killer. . . .

He dropped onto the sofa and stared up at the rafters, at the forest of antlers that wavered in the dancing light from the fireplace. He thought of what he
was. Alone. Isolated. The way he'd always felt. But
now he had a time of real need. Who in God's name
could he possibly talk to?

Joannie? The one human meaning ever in his life,
as deep in him as the roots of his beginnings. . . .
He looked into the fire, keeping his vigil. For the
memory of her. For the killer's next move.

Once, in the midst of a half-sleep with his eyes
open, he saw a man—himself?—framed in front of the
window in the back bunkroom, a girl on her knees at
his feet. He looked closer, saw that the man was a
stranger, a tall man in a carefully tailored suit, handsome, well-cut hair and manicured fingernails, a self-
assured man of culture and good breeding. The girl
kneeling at his feet was Joannie—

He started, wide awake. The fire was dying. The

room was black and cold, and he was sweating. Wake someone else, he thought, but he knew he couldn't sleep. If they slept now, at least they all slept. The killer had to be as exhausted as the rest of them. He couldn't possibly lie in a bunk with no coffee and keep himself awake. It wasn't human. And the killer couldn't wake up without hearing something, which they'd all hear. . . . Norm willed himself to think. If he didn't sleep, what would he be like in the morning . . . how alert, or fast? If he did sleep, would there be any morning?

For a long time he sat there. Once he jerked his head, knowing he'd been dozing. He couldn't keep this up. He got up quietly and gathered some pillows and jackets from other chairs and arranged them under a blanket on the sofa where he usually slept. Taking a pillow, some more blankets and socks and his winter jacket, he padded into the kitchen and worked his way in behind and underneath the dining table. The hard, cold floor bore sharply, like a bed of nails, against the soreness of his body. But here he could see and hear in the dark, and no one would know where he was. It would be relatively safe. At least he could sleep. He had to.

Within minutes his mind numbed, aware dimly of the others snoring away in the back bunkroom, of the raging storm that had almost taken their lives, of the isolation of this shack in the wilderness—and his own isolation inside it.

CHAPTER XX

He couldn't breathe. Something was clogging his throat, mouth, lungs. He stirred, then almost dozed, sank back into his bed. . . . Someone close by coughed. He waved his arm, pushing the blanket off his face. It would not move. Abruptly he rolled sideways, banging his head against a hard object. Lights flashed, a bright flickering stabbed into his eyes, dark clouds billowing above. That coughing again. Heat, suffocation filling his throat and lungs. A burning sensation. "What—?" He sat up, banging his head again, rolling back and blinking through a forest of obscuring trees between him and the dancing lights surrounding him on every side . . . the trees, the table, surrounding chairs—he was under the table, and they were burning. . . .

He pawed his way through the legs of the table and chairs, headed for the nearby door. Someone choked, a dry, hacking sound. He reached the base of the door, reached up into the black smoke, grabbed hold of the knob and pulled . . . the door gave only a fraction, as if held from the outside. "Hey, hey," he yelled, startled by the high pitch of his voice. "*Hey.*" he pulled mightily, one foot braced against the wall, his head buried in the choking black smoke. Outside the wooden planking he could swear he detected movement and heavy breathing . . . and someone giggling?

"No." He fell back to the floor, hugging the planking for what little air was available. He was going to burn up in here.

The thought collected him. The world became crystal clear. The killer stood outside the door, and they were all going to burn so that the killer would go free.

Quickly, driven by the heat, he burrowed his way underneath the tables and chairs, bulling his way between chair legs, gathering up the blanket and his overcoat as he passed, aware that to dive through the front window in his underwear would only mean he'd freeze instead of burn. Chin low to the floor and hugging to the front of the cabin, he scurried along the wall and grabbed at a pile of clothes on a chair. He half stood into the searing heat of black smoke and felt in the dark for his rifle, lowest on the rack. It was still there. The weapon in hand, he grabbed for a pair of boots beside the chair, then, on knees and one elbow, his booty bundled together in one arm, he felt along the wall for the front picture window. The glass was hot. He crawled back toward the flames, coughing. His eyes streamed tears from the smoke, and he squinted to maintain a fix on the window so he would not hurtle head first into the wall. Something burned his left hip. He looked down to see flames working at his long underwear and the corners of his blanket. He held the bundle of clothes, boots and rifle to his belly, the rifle pointing straight ahead, the blanket thrust out in front of him. He half stood, then ran into the wall of dense black smoke.

Splinters of thick glass flew as he rolled forward in the cold of deep white snow, flames still on his underwear and blanket. He rolled sideways, smothering them. The flames of the cabin behind him were shooting up twenty feet into the night. He thought he heard voices inside but he couldn't be sure.

Someone appeared at the corner of the cabin, medium-built, face distorted in the unsteady light of the flames.

Glenn.

Norm scrambled to his feet, reaching for the bundle of boots and clothes and clutching his rifle. At the corner Glenn turned away, and then suddenly back, a rifle in hand. Norm's legs seemed to churn in the slow motion of a bad dream as his stockinged feet pumped up and down in the snow to get him away from the light of the flames. He was getting nowhere. He saw Glenn's rifle come up, pitched himself forward in the deep snow an instant before the gun went off.

A second explosion. He managed three loping paces before the sound of a third shot again sent him rolling half naked in the snow.

He cut in behind a tree to shield himself from view, driving further into the trees, the flickering light from the flames making the whole forest appear to dance. Halfway up a slope his lungs gave out and he leaned against a tree, coughing and wheezing, trying to look back in the direction of the towering flames to see if Glenn had followed.

Flames now engulfed the entire cabin. In front of the shack a ball of flame materialized, moving slowly away. A high-pitched wail, one seemingly filled more with anger than pain, straightened Norm's back. Slowly the figure moved out, arms waving helplessly, trying to fend off the flames, the huge body bending, staggering, then toppling backward into the snow, rolling, arms and legs twitching outward, unable to smother them completely. Eventually the body stopped wailing, stopped moving, one arm lifted up as if to wave, then dropped into the snow to lie still.

Only the flames continued—on the body, and in the cabin.

Norm turned away.

After several moments he turned back. The storm had, if anything, gotten worse, but the heavy snow did nothing to slow the flames. The wind was driving the snow almost horizontally. He shivered. Quickly, walking back through the forest, he slipped on his red-and-black-checkered over-coat, then his pants. He discovered he had lost one boot somewhere, either inside the shack or in the snow between.

"Easy now," he told himself. He wasn't finished yet. His hunting cap and gloves were in his coat pocket, and the remains of the charred blanket, tightly wrapped and tied around his foot, would protect him for now. He moved over and settled in, using a thick tree trunk as a windbreak while he waited to see if the killer . . . if *Glenn* . . . would trail him while he waited on the dawn. . . .

Glenn? The most solid of them all . . . ?

He laid his rifle across his legs, remembering how the fire's heat had scalded his lungs, the way the smoke had blinded and nearly suffocated him in its death squeeze. "I'm at you, Glenn," he muttered aloud. He could hear the disbelief in his own voice . . . Glenn, the most solid of them all. . . .

Shells, he thought in the next instant. In his hurry he'd forgotten to grab shells. He felt in his coat pocket. He had shells, all right.

But only two.

The storm swallowed the dawn whole. With the snow and low dark clouds, the best nature could muster was a weak twilight in which Glenn could barely see to move. Forget about seeing into the shadows of the thickets of trees and brush. After spending the night camped in the forest behind the charred re-

mains of the shack he was on the move, slogging
toward the seven-mile swamp.

Such a night, the best of plans. . . . Hour after
hour struggling to stay awake. And then creeping
through the cold shack, the blackness so complete
that he couldn't see his own hand, which held the
Luger in case Norm showed up. But nothing had
moved and he had escaped outside undetected, so he
could block the front door and start his fire with
kerosene from the lamp. . . .

"I don't know how I escaped," he imagined saying
to the authorities, holding up the blistered left arm
he'd purposely held in the flames. "As I said, we were
all exhausted. When I woke up the shack was completely in flames. I grabbed my clothes off a chair and
dove out the window. I guess no one else woke up in
time. I should have gone back." Barbara would pat
him on the shoulder, and his father would tell him
he'd done just fine, he was proud of him and he
should be thankful he'd survived. . . .

He'd thought all this through as he stood there after setting the clothes on his left arm on fire,
watching the flames burning at the cloth, searing his
flesh, watching the flames as they spread through the
shack. He'd had no choice, after all . . . they'd
forced his hand by believing Norm . . .
Norm. . . .

A loud crash of glass, he'd turned to see a body
rolling in the snow, then had whirled away, diving to
his belly, left arm smothered beneath him. He got up
once but the flames started again and he lay quickly
on his arm to smother them, then vaulted up and
seized the rifle and whirled back on Norm, pointing
and firing. But the big man, rolling in the snow, his
arms filled with clothes and his rifle jutting out from
one side, somehow managed to escape into the trees.
Without moving a step he'd slumped down, cross-
legged in the snow beside the burning shack, fingers

of heat scalding at his face. A huge ball of flame, Butch he figured, emerged from the shack, bellowing, staggering, falling, rolling, then lying still, the flames still eating. He hadn't blinked. . . . It was coming down to what he'd wanted from the start . . . Glenn and Norm. Glenn against Norm. . . . Good old always so strong and *understanding* Norm. . . .

All that had been hours ago, ages ago. He moved with purpose now, certain that Norm had survived the night, that the big man, no doubt lying in ambush all night long, would soon be on the trail in pursuit.

But just as certain as he was of Norm's ability to survive the night, he also knew Norm had to be sapped . . . dragging the big black out of the swamp, dragging Merald in the storm, weakened from the bullet in his arm. And now he'd push the big man further, make him flounder through the deep snow and the storm to track him down.

He allowed himself a grin, his mind completely filled with his new plan. It was the big man's way, to pick up his trail, to zigzag in and out, using his body, watching his flanks. The big hunter exhausting himself.

"Oh, Norman," Glenn said into the storm, a father admonishing his child's foolishness. Now he would use the cornerstone of Norm's hunting creed, patience. "Patience," Norm had preached over and over years ago when Glenn had first joined the shack. "That'll get you more game than anything else, patience." And now it would kill him. His skill and knowledge would kill him.

He toiled along the base of the high ridge, eventually turning and ascending the saddle which they normally climbed to the top. But halfway up he made an abrupt left, back along the side of the ridge toward the shack, then went part of the way down the hill so

he could see the base of the saddle where his trail
started upward. One last time, Norm . . . it was
there that Norm, sooner or later, was obliged to circle
back in order to confirm that his quarry had
indeed climbed the ridge. Of course Norm wouldn't
follow his trail up the saddle, Glenn knew. But he
would have to return to that junction at the base of
the ridge in order to see which way the tracks turned.
And there, finally, the big man would die. . . .

Glenn settled in behind a fallen oak, a thicket of
leafless hazel brush protecting his back. He hunched
forward, hands in his pockets, the hood pulled tight
around his face as the wind and driven snow slashed
unnoticed at him.

He waited.

Reluctantly, in the dim gray of the dawn, Norm
roused himself from behind the enclave of balsams,
moving against the cold and stiffness that froze his
muscles. He grunted as sharp knives bore up from
where he'd been burned, and from his arm where
he'd been shot. Slowly on stiff legs he shuffled forward, moving carefully to keep the blanket wrapped
around his foot, eyes probing to the side, front and
rear.

The hunting shack was gone, only a flattened pile
of charred timbers and the rock fireplace remaining,
a few trickles of smoke making their way upward to
join the storm. In a few hours it would be concealed
by white, and by spring grown over by weeds and
brush.

Norm paused, crouched beside a tree at the edge of
the clearing. To the right lay the charred, snow-covered hump of the body, and beyond that, Butch's
jeep. Ten feet in front of him he spotted what appeared to be the edge of his boot sticking above the
snow. He waited, watching but seeing nothing. He

rushed out, seized the boot, and darted back behind the tree.

He circled the burnt cabin at a distance and moved up through the brush. To one side of where the shack had been he saw the four deer still suspended from the hanging pole. The big black stood out clearly from the others, huge, snow-covered, a frozen and forgotten carcass that bore no resemblance to the noble creature he'd once thought it to be. Dead, by his hand.

He turned and sank back into the darkness of the forest, thinking that in the space of a heartbeat he could be no more than that pitiful remnant of the big black.

Well, maybe that would be for the best . . . at least it would end right—up here in the northwoods that he loved best. . . .

The darkness of the day served only to show the thickness of the clouds and the heaviness of the horizontal flight of the snow, a darkness worse than night because of the illusion, the apparent ability to see, and yet the blurred confusion scant yards away in the thick brush. A man moving in the open would be spotlighted, a figure stilled in the brush unseen.

He stepped forward, aware of a feeling he'd last known in Korea, also the last time he'd hunted a human being. His mind clicked steadily: terrain, weather, the time lag since the fire, his quarry—Glenn. He moved slowly, with deliberation, picking the thickest terrain, never mind the difficulty of movement.

First he'd make a wide circle around the shack, pinpoint if Glenn remained in the immediate area, perhaps even circle behind Glenn as he lay in wait. Glenn was against it now, damn him . . . little chance of a back shot now. He fervently hoped the bastard realized it.

He pressed on, almost eagerly, checking all around,

moving despite the angry bite of his burns, the ache in his arm, the soreness in his legs. He ducked under snow-covered limbs, sometimes half squatting to thread his way through the thickest available cover, bending, squinting, picking over the terrain as carefully as a beaver surveying a dam site.

He almost stepped on the tracks before he saw them, a sobering reminder of the restricted visibility. The indent in the light, fluffy snow was clear, but how old he could not say for sure—a good while, at least—moving away from the shack and moving fast. He stared through the blizzard toward the swamp and the high unseen ridge that bordered one side. The freezing bite of the blizzard cut into his flesh, a reminder of what could lie ahead. The tracks receded into the forest, drawing him on as if their maker were certain he'd follow. And he would. He felt a certain pleasure mixed with fear that Glenn knew him that well.

The tracks, of course, were a trap. He made a wide S-pattern, curving fifty to a hundred yards out and then back, snaking between the ridge and the swamp, crossing the tracks every fifteen minutes or so.

At first the soreness of his body obliged him to move slowly, holding his rifle with the safety off, ready for instant use.

In time, the stiffness of his body eased. The wind blew at a steady twenty miles per hour, gusting well over thirty. To stop was also to die, he knew, and he maintained his pace in the half-light. A hunter would be forced to close very near his quarry on such a day, and fire quickly and without a scope. He paused, shielded in an enclave of balsams, and, with a smooth effortless motion despite the bite of pain in his arm, raised his rifle, the iron sights, bead and vee beneath his scope automatically lining up as the stock touched his cheek. Snow or not, he could shoot. Better than a man with only a scope.

Moments later, on his circle back toward the ridge to double check the trail, he could not find the tracks. Back and back he circled, his movement slowed, searching all around until he spotted the tracks leading up into the deep ridge saddle, a canyon from which he could be ambushed from any one of three sides. Surely Glenn didn't think him that stupid, he thought. One thing certain, the man held the high ground. . . .

He sighed at the thought of the long climb up that steep ridge. His strength was fading again, he knew, checking his back trail. There. A figure, a dark outline barely visible through the dim light and flying snow and thin line of hazel brush. He watched as the figure raised the rifle and slipped in behind the covering shadow of the trees. But no crash of a bullet, no report from a rifle, just the continuing woosh of the wind and snow lashing the cowering forest.

He knelt in the snow, shoulder pressed against the trunk of a pine. He'd been certain Glenn was on the ridge. But again he'd been fooled. Again and again and again. He was a hunter, one of the best, he'd once thought, and all these times he'd been surprised. Like most everything else in his life . . . a self-made illusion.

Keeping his body behind the tree trunk and his head concealed as best he could behind pine boughs, he peered out to where the man had been. Nothing. Whatever, he reminded himself, he had only two shells, two chances.

He shifted to better see his flanks in case the man circled, surveying the terrain as he would a deer crossing, determining exactly where the man could move undetected, where he'd be exposed. The sight of the killer had flushed his body with warmth, despite the freezing bite of the wind. There, there, and there, he thought, memorizing the different avenues of approach. If he could stay alert, patient and watchful, the man couldn't touch him without being seen. Except from up on the ridge, he corrected himself, but with the deep snow that would take Glenn a long time to travel across. Still he turned, suddenly sensing something awry in his logic. And there, far up the ridge, were a head, shoulders and a rifle, thrust out from behind a fallen tree.

Move—Norm's mind screamed at him, the defense of a deer—move. As fast as he could he rose out of his crouch, surging forward and crashing through the small grove of balsams. He heard the shot, distant, muffled by the storm. Safe, he thought, as the wall of trees closed behind him. But ahead and off to his right the outline of a *second* man turned in his direction, rifle slowly pulling around and pointing at his position. Norm veered to the left with surprising speed through the drifts, dodging trees and crashing through brush like an escaping deer. Three more shots, much closer and louder than the last, bullets snapping through the brush and cracking angrily past his head.

Faster, a buck with its head back in flight, bounding in long, low leaps through the trees and deadfalls, a desperate rush to save its life. He continued to run long after he'd passed deep enough into the forest to be concealed, his momentum carrying him fifty, a hundred yards before he made a small fishhook and slumped in behind a deadfall where he could watch his backtrail. He shook his head, straining for breath, chest heaving. "Son of a bitch." Two of them. At least two of them. Almost, but not quite fast or accurate enough. Not quite. He stared through the white haze of the snowy forest, his brown eyes darting back and forth.

After a few minutes he regained his breath, but his high ebbed, replaced by a deep weariness, and puzzlement.

It was impossible, he knew. But they were there.

A gray hint of movement drew his attention, a figure filtering through the brush, following exactly on the path he'd run along. That after all this the man could be so careless or ignorant. . . .

He aimed across the broad base of the deadfall, his forearm steadied on the tree, a sure hit when the man came out of the brush. The figure dragged itself closer, seeming once or twice to stumble, to stagger sideways and lean against a tree. He brought his sights to bear on the dark outline. He could make out the legs clearly now beneath the browse line. *A man*, Norm . . . His throat became dry, tongue sticking to the roof of his mouth. *One of his own kind.* . . . He touched at the curve of the trigger, forcing hmself to recall the shots minutes before buzzing past his head, the dead hunter in the forest, the burning figure staggering out into the snow, the shot ripping through his arm as he dreamt of Joannie. . . . He hunched forward, squinting down his sight, body tensed slightly, finger squeezing, squeezing—

The recoil of the rifle surprised him.

"No," he said as if wishing to call back what he'd done. But it was too late; the figure had crumpled sideways, his legs chopped from beneath, a sledge hammer driving him into the snow.

Cautiously he stood and circled the deadfall and moved forward, searching all around as he moved. Nausea gathered in his throat, the throbbing at his temples making him dizzy. He'd just killed a man, but a man hunting him, he thought with forced satisfaction.

Faster and faster he moved forward, compelled by an awful curiosity to see what he'd done—

"*Rod*," he said in wonderment, and stopped. He stared down. It was Rod all right, but only half-dressed, a winter coat and gloves—no hat, long underwear and pants, wool socks caked with snow and no boots. There were flecks of blood for ten feet beyond where he'd fallen. "Rod," Norm called again, and knelt in the snow.

Rod's eyes flickered open. His thin, blued face moved as if he was about to speak, but he only shivered.

"Why?" Norm asked, cradling Rod's icy blond curls in his arm. "What the hell were you after me for?"

"Burning, burning," Rod mumbled through shivering teeth, his eyes clenched shut. "Burning. You burned us."

"What? . . . No," Norm protested. "No, not me."

But Rod lay still now, the flesh of his handsome face sagging. Norm looked down at his pale, almost blue face, at the multiple burn marks on the coat and the long underwear, at the caked ice and snow on the bootless, stockinged feet. He recalled the man staggering as he followed his tracks. Burns and frozen feet and no pants and still he came.

Gently, Norm laid Rod's head back in the snow. He checked Rod's pockets and rifle, discovering the rifle was empty. Completely empty and still he'd followed. He must have been delirious. Norm glanced **around the** forest, then back at the body. Such a small man. And for a moment there, as he'd lined up on the outline of the figure, he'd actually felt a sense of elation. He winced, rubbing his hand across his face. Not thinking, he fastened the bottom two buttons on Rod's coat and pulled the collar up around Rod's head. He stood up, staring out through the forest toward the ridge, toward where Glenn lay in wait.

CHAPTER XXI

It'd taken so long to clear his fogged and snow-covered scope. And then, just as he lined up on Norm, squeezing at the trigger, the big man had spotted him again and gotten away. Out of the storm, off to the right, three more shots in the wind. And then nothing, the wind and the snow howling and rattling in his ears, minutes passing as he wondered whether he'd really heard those last three shots. Then *another* shot, then nothing.

What in the world . . . ? He rocked back and forth. Eventually, seeing nothing, he stood up, exposed to whomever might be concealed down below in the gray haze. He started down the slope, going faster and faster until his inclined body was too far ahead of his legs and he pitched headlong into the snow. He lay there, panting, his head buried. And for a moment he just lay there, his thoughts drifting like the snow, being taken over by the cold and the fatigue. . . . "Good morning, Glenn," Barbara was saying and bending for her kiss on the cheek, setting the two poached eggs on dry toast in front of him, the glass of fresh squeezed orange juice—his one self-indulgence—black coffee already in place. "Did you sleep well?" And he, nodding his head, eyes fixed on the yellow of the egg yolk as he neatly punctured it with his fork, watched it run over the toast, patted the slime with a spoon, knowing Barbara would turn away. . . . Breakfast complete, and so to work, a three-mile drive to his clinic. . . . Three chairs, one for Mrs. Maynard his hygienist's patients, the other two completely equipped for his, instruments cleaned and laid out as prescribed as he walked in the door. . . . "Good morning," in a firm, friendly tone, and while he washed his hands, his first patient was efficiently set up in room number one, and he walked in, checking the patient's card for name and giving his greeting. . . . "Good morning, Norm. . . ."

Good-by, Norm. He struggled up out of the snow, wiping at his face, rifle dangling from one hand, the barrel and scope clogged with snow. Three shots *after* his, and then one later on?

He picked up the track where Norm had run, little indentations in the snow. If he hadn't seen Norm moving he wouldn't be able to tell which way they went. He pushed ahead, bobbing his head when a second trail joined in with Norm's. His pace quickened. There, a mound in the snow. He walked up. Rod. Dressed in the bottoms of his long underwear and a winter jacket. No boots or hat. He knelt down, saw the blood, and the bullet hole in Rod's chest. He stared out at the dark of the forest, at the black shadows and darkened tree trunks, at the white haze of snow filtering everywhere. The wind drove through the nylon of his jacket and he shivered, the sweat from his rapid movements turning to ice. Rod had escaped from the fire, and Norm had just killed him. . . .

He marveled at the clarity of his thinking, even managed the hint of a smile. Norm killed Rod. And Norm fired the shack, he'd tell them. "We were hunting up in that area where that one hunter got killed the other day. We didn't even know about it until we went into Swede's that same day. And we didn't really connect Norm to it until later, when we got to talking about those other killings in previous years. Norm . . . poor fellow, maybe he figured he was taking his stand with the deer or some such thing. . . . He *was* getting that way, you know. Couldn't even bear to shoot anything anymore, except for that eighteen-pointer, all by himself out in the seven-mile swamp. Yessir. Probably felt it was doomed anyway, and better the great hunter Norm kill it than poor Rod or Butch or one of us mere mortals. . . ." It was a good story and that last part might even be true. He was quite pleased with himself.

So one man was left, a dentist from Des Plaines, his left arm burned through. And old Norm, the killer.

He laughed aloud into the storm and shook his head. Besides, Norm wanted to die up here in the wilds. Everyone knew his life at the factory and with Joannie was finished. It was here in the forest that old Norm really came alive. He'd said that often enough. And here he'd die.

"Nature's way," Glenn said, echoing Norm's favorite words as he brushed snow from his rifle. He cleaned his scope and held the rifle up to check it, again wiping off the snow and slipping his lens cover over the ends. He stepped forward, rifle held ready, following directly in Norm's tracks, figuring out just what Norm, the killer of four innocent hunters, would do.

Norm moved slowly along the edge of the seven-mile swamp, seeing Rod's diminutive body at his feet, crystals of snow steadily mounting on Rod's clothing and face, flecks of white shamelessly covering all that they touched. His feet continued their ponderous up-and-down movement, the burn in his hip wearing deeper and deeper, the wound in his arm oozing blood, the slashing wind and snow blunted only slightly by the soft wool of his hunting clothes. He gazed at the white nothingness of the sky, too aware that he had just killed an unarmed man. But he plodded ahead, with his one bullet, his slitted eyes probing the storm and the thickets. He was still a man on the hunt. For survival.

Once he paused, leaning beside a large poplar. The huge trunk moved, swaying with the push of the wind, rolling gracefully in the throes of nature's fury. He looked at the shield of bark inches from his face, the tan-green areas smooth like a sheen of plastic, the rough black areas scarred from years of struggle. It was a good tree, he thought, solid. A survivor.

He looked at the snow clinging to his wool clothes from head to foot. It was a strange substance, tiny crystals of ice formed into beautifully intricate patterns, if one looked closely. He reached down and formed a small ball of snow and bit into it, trying to ease his thirst.

One way or the other, here and now, it had to be resolved. All of it. . . .

He concentrated, figuring as he'd figured a buck. Rod's shots in the valley . . . Glenn would have a time figuring that out. And he could not simply let him be, Norm knew. His attempts in the past proved that. Norm looked back toward Rod's unseen form. "He'll be along," he said out loud. "He'll be along. He has to."

He moved down along the scattered brush and saplings of the highland flat, crowding the tangled thickets of the seven-mile swamp, eventually circling down into it and well out into the thickets, then circling back to parallel his own track made after he'd left Rod's body.

As he worked his way into the first part of the swamp, the swaying hemlock trees and balsams

blocked the wind and the green-needled limbs
blunted the drive of the snow, creating the illusion
that the storm was letting up. Still the wind howled
above and his movement through the entanglements
were much more painful and slower than he'd anticipated. And the world of white with no sign of the sun
made knowing his direction a difficult task. One lax
moment and he could easily circle out too far, or in
too close, and run into Glenn face to face.

Time passed. He neared the edge of the swamp. He
paused, peering through the storm toward the slight
uplift of the highland. Surely his tracks were right up
there. Surely Glenn must move along here. It was
midday but dark as dusk. The wind continued strong
as ever, swirling snow and lowering visibility to a
matter of feet. He hesitated, uncertain of the length
of time of his circling, the location of his passing
tracks unclear. He closed his eyes, trying to concentrate.

"It has to be right," he mumbled, the decision
made. He cast about and found the huge gray stump
of a three-foot-thick pine tree, a remnant of virgin
timber from the turn of the century. He pressed in
behind the stump, watching the high land, standing
in a small hollow, his back to the wind, head and
shoulders showing above the stump. He hunched his
shoulders against the cold, thrust his gloved hands
into his coat pocket, and began his vigil.

Within an hour a deep chill had worked into his
bones. At times he would stand quietly, hunched forward into the warmth of himself, then abruptly
breaking against the strain and shivering violently.
Even his mind felt cold, aware only of the chills racking his body and the need to at least be on the lookout.

If he'd checked his flanks and rear once, he'd
checked them five hundred times, each time without
result. To turn was to disturb his clothes and muscles

knotted against the driving cold. In time he checked his flanks and rear less often, relying instead on an intuitive feel for what lay behind him, on an in-built awareness. He'd have to depend on it to sense an alien presence, movement. . . . After all, this was where he lived, always had. He hoped it would give him an edge. . . .

Abruptly, by sense or chance, he had no time to decide, he turned and saw the shadow of a shockingly nearby figure. For a stilled fraction of a second they did not move. The instant was concentrated; the figure enshrouded in a hooded, snow-covered bundle of clothing.

Norm watched, his back against the jagged stump, snow clinging to his woolen clothes, a misshapen snowman, inanimate except for the light of his dark eyes. And the picture clicked . . . a time years before when a buck had accidentally walked up behind him. In a movement so quick the buck could only widen its eyes in terror, he'd whirled and fired and dropped the buck dead in its tracks. But not this time, not with only one bullet. He whirled now to put the stump between himself and the figure, the corner of his eye glimpsing a snow flurry of motion.

Two shots came close together and chunks of pine pitch splattered out of the stump, one piece stinging Norm's cheek. Momentarily he ducked down behind the stump, vaulting sideways after the second blast. A dimly seen figure was diving through the curtain of snow and saplings as he thrust his rifle around one side of the stump, the bead and vee falling into place and searching through the screen of saplings for the man scrambling sideways on his hands and knees. No, he thought. One bullet—it had to be good.

He pulled back. The world came clear, the weathered gray surface of the huge trunk scant inches from his face, the round hard snowflakes bouncing off the stock of his rifle, the wind cutting through the saplings. It was here, all of it, including Glenn fifty feet away. A hunt. But to hunt he had to kill. It was a rule.

"Glenn." He yelled the name over the gray stump, his words carried off in the wind. "Glenn . . . can you hear me?"

"I hear you, Norm." Glenn's voice came through in its calm tone. Good morning, Norm, open wide, please. . . .

"They're all dead. Rod, Butch, Bernie . . . all of them. . . ."

"You killed Rod," Glenn said, concealed behind another stump.

"He shot at me, I thought he was you . . . but you and your fire brought him out here, Glenn. . . ." He took a deep breath. Silence.

"Can you *understand*, Glenn? They're dead."

The dentist became irritated. The patient should shut his mouth. "I heard you . . . so they're dead."

"Glenn, you need help."

Glenn laughed. Doctor knew best. "No, Norm. *You* need help. Ask the others—"

"You killed the other . . . all those so-called accidents—"

"Yep," Glenn said, proud of his work.

"My god," Norm said, as much to himself as to Glenn, "what the hell for?"

"Oh, Norm," Glenn said, "you won't be the only one to ask that." He caught his breath, pleasure clear in his tone. "They'll all be asking that. They'd never figure someone like me for this. And even if you could live to tell them they'd never believe it—from you or anyone. Not about Glenny."

"They? Who the hell—"

"They?" Glenn was loud with hilarity now. "*They* . . . everyone . . . dad, Barbara. All of 'em, they *know* me. They tell me what to do . . . all my life, Glenn do this, Glenn do that, Glenn behave yourself. . . . And I *have*, Norm, I *have*. Haven't I, Norm? Well, damn you, haven't I?" And he slammed three shots into Norm's stump, one bullet bursting through just in front of Norm's face, tiny pieces of pine pitch stinging his cheek.

"Take it easy, Glenn—"

A shot. "Take it *easy* your *fucking* self," Glenn yelled back. "All my life they tell me to take it easy, take it easy. Well, dammit to hell, I'm taking it easy . . . I'm taking *you* easy, Norm, just like the others. No sweat, no sweat at all. . . ."

"Glenn," Norm said, trying to be calm, trying to cut through the man's rage. "We didn't all die in the fire. There's too much evidence now. . . . Rod, me . . . it's all over with—"

"Oh, Norm. That's good. All over with. You're right, Norm, just like always. . . . I've got to admit you had me worried, though. Twice you got away from me. Twice. That's pretty good, Norm—"

"Let's give it up, Glenn. . . . I don't want to kill you and you don't really want to kill me—"

"Well, then, Norm, old buddy, just stand up and come on over and we'll smoke the old peace pipe. . . ."

Norm felt the weariness of all the past days bearing down. "You don't care about life, do you, Glenn? I mean, do you realize you've been killing human beings?"

"Norm," Glenn said, the amusement still in his voice, "I like you. You know that. I've always liked you better than the others. Rod and his ego, Butch and his loud bluster, Merald and his damn money, brokendown Bernie and his booze. . . . When you come right down to it, Norm, they were a pretty sad lot. No loss, really. But you, you've got character, Norm, you know what's right. You're a real man, Norm, old buddy. . . ."

"But you'd still kill me as easy as the others—"

"Well, sure. I'm a man too. It's you or me. What do you expect? Besides, after you I'm all done hunting. I'm going home, take it easy . . . do what they want me to. . . ." His voice was beginning to sag.

"For God's sake, Glenn, think. There's too much evidence. There are bodies all over the place. They'll know what you've done—"

"What *I've* done? What *you've* done, Norm. You shot Rod. You set the fire. You killed the others. But I managed to live and I hunted you down."

Norm pressed his head against the stump.

"You'll like it better this way, Norm. You don't have anything to go back to anyway. This way you can stay up here in your woods with your squirrels and chickadees and that nice big eighteen-pointer you shot just to stick in Rod's face. It's all for the best, Norm. The way it should be. You get what you want, and I get what I want."

His temples throbbed. Silently as he could, facing the stump and keeping it between himself and Glenn, he backed away, laboring through the deep snow, bent over in a crouch, rifle ready. When he judged himself out of sight, he turned and moved deeper into the slashings, starting to circle in a lumbering trot, a move designed to bring him quickly to his foe's flank with the advantage of surprise.

But halfway around the circle he was forced to slow down, gasping for breath. No sound from Glenn. He could have moved too, perhaps as quickly as he.

Norm crouched, still fighting for air, surveying the brush around him. If he stayed motionless, the surprise he'd gained in his run would ebb away. In a blurred terrain of waving saplings and blowing snow the outline of movement was most vulnerable, he knew, especially if the observer remained well-concealed and alert. Still, he could not remain entrenched forever, if for no other reason than to keep from freezing to death.

He neared the flank of the stump Glenn had ducked behind, reasonably sure of his sense of distance and direction in spite of the swirling storm . . . years of experience were worth something. He edged forward in a crouch, his breathing labored but controlled, his hands tensed, not tight but firm, a controlled readiness. Gradually, as though out of a fog, the outline of the stump emerged, a gray piece of wood. And no Glenn.

He looked from side to side for what could not be seen. He sank to his knees, feeling the exhaustion, crushed by a sense of failure, an old man's awareness that he could no longer perform. To die was all he had left—

But he shook off the depression. The stump was the right one—he'd been correct, the proof lying there in the tracks that were already filling with blowing snow. Glenn had been here and had left, circling in the opposite direction from him .The uncontrollable part of any hunt, the element of chance . . . it had to be one way or the other. Glenn had simply managed to guess correctly this time.

He turned back toward the stump where he'd taken refuge himself. It was simply a matter of time.

Again luck seemed to intervene, and spurred by the hint of movement or some inner awareness, he glanced to his right directly at the shadow of Glenn, who'd cut his circuit too short and circled back in front of his own stump.

Features all but obliterated by his hood and the covering storm, Glenn grunted in surprise but was already preparing his rifle to shoot.

Norm moved as he'd learned in Korea—no matter what, get in the first shot. His body turned, rifle leveled before it touched his shoulder, both eyes on the target, drawing the barrel into line with the eyes, an instinctive lining-up.

He knew he'd missed even as he squeezed. Glenn's

wild, headlong dive pulling him just out of the sight picture as the rifle went off. "Jesus, no," Norm moaned, his last bullet spent uselessly in the storm.

Like a panic-stricken crab, Glenn scrambled on hands and knees through the deep snow. Clawing and flailing through the snow and brush, rising up and reeling sideways, legs churning, crashing into a small tree and tumbling into the snow. He stared back through the brush and storm toward Norm's outline, waiting for the final bullet.

But it didn't come. Norm stayed on his knees, rifle dangling from one hand. Still scrambling, Glenn saw Norm get up and turn away. Glenn whirled back, raising his rifle and fumbling for the trigger. Nothing. He glanced down, seeing the bolt cocked open, the clip spent. He fumbled in his coat pocket for his other clip. Nothing. They must have dropped when he dived into the snow.

He glanced up. Norm had disappeared. But Norm was his now.

"I know you're out of shells, Norm. I'm coming after you," he shouted into the wind. He took out the black Luger, checking to be sure a shell was chambered, and clicked the safety off. Gently he set his rifle down, leaning it against a tree, and went off after Norm.

"The end is near, Norm," he said gaily into the storm. "You know I'm in shape. You know you're exhausted. Give it up." No answer, except the steadily blowing storm.

He found Norm's trail easily, an eighteen-inch-wide indentation in the snow, the snow at the bottom falling back in to be a foot deep. From the trail alone the direction of movement was impossible to decipher, but Glenn had seen where Norm stood, and he set out in his wake, pistol held in front of him as he snaked through thick brush. A man could lie concealed in here as well as in a jungle. He played the muzzle of the pistol back and forth across the brush, ready for that one shot into Norm's big chest. Point-blank, like Norm, or they, could never imagine possible. . . .

After some time the furrow of Norm's track abruptly separated. Glenn halted. Norm had circled back into his own track and then split off again. But which way? Glenn gazed up at the white of the sky blending with the white of the snow and then with the gray haze of the forest. The stumps. Which way were the stumps? There? Did Norm go back this way? Which tracks had the most snow in them? They would be the oldest. He peered closely, deciding first on one and then the other.

There, a shadow of movement. He fired the Luger once. The wind blew, gusting, a clump of snow falling off a balsam limb, a shadow.

"Die, Norm," he yelled, straining to force the words past lips drawn tight by rage . . . rage draining him. . . . He shook his head . . . they just had no idea what kind of Glenn they were dealing with, the poor damn fools. . . .

He chose the left fork, but the choice didn't really matter . . . sooner or later Norm would run out of strength, sooner or later he'd find the big man and that would be that and . . . "take that," he'd say and push the barrel in their faces, laughing at their surprise, their fear. . . . "Why, *Glenny*," they'd whine. And "Glenny, *Glenny*," Glenn chanted, choking, laughing as he made his way through the thickets of the seven-mile swamp. The furrow circled, he could feel, coming back in on the furrow of another trail. Left or right? He fired a shot to the left and started out to the right, moving faster now, intent on running Norm into the ground. . . .

A few minutes of this and his breathing had become ragged, sweat streamed from his armpits as he hurried through the tangle of little circles. With each circle he moved faster, sure that sooner or later Norm would screw up, and that he'd catch sight of him, run right up to him and "pow, pow, pow. . . ." "But *Glenny*, why?" his high-pitched voice once again mimicking their whine.

He paused. Again the tracks forked, this time heading out in three directions. Obviously Norm had been here twice before. He smiled and backed in behind an uprooted balsam, his eye on the fork. "Make it three times, Norm. . . ."

The cold wind blew steadily, cutting through his clothes, chilling his sweat. His teeth actually rattled. Patience, he thought, Norm's creed. Turn it around, use it against him. . . .

He shook violently, movement he could not control. Maybe Norm had returned to the high land. He looked around. One direction appeared exactly like the other. That's how the seven-mile swamp was in a storm. . . .

His breath shortened. Something popped, a clearing inside his head. He stared down at the separating furrows in the snow, stepped back to the trail, and to the side of one furrow he bent a limb as a marker. He set out on one track, his shivering subsumed in the act, his eyes on the track and the swamp.

Within fifty yards he realized that the track was not circling back to the others, it was going in a straight line away from the area of the stumps.

Norm was trying to escape. He had him now.

"Watch this," he said out loud.

The tracks led into an open area and through some marsh grass to a swamp creek where Norm's tracks showed he'd inched sideways across a log to cross the black open water of the six-feet-wide creek. He moved forward through the fluffed-up snow beside the creek, intent on taking one step on the packed-down snow

in the middle of the log, then vaulting on across to
the opposite—

A loud crack ripped the air like a rifle shot, the log
splitting in two and tumbling him sideways into the
three-feet-deep water. He boiled upward, coughing,
sputtering, pistol in hand. He saw it instantly. The
log wasn't complete. It was an old gray thing about
ten inches in diameter, but only three or so inches
thick, the top part of a hollow log, the bottom eaten
away from lying in the swamp. Norm must have
walked on it on land, then picked it up and laid it
across the stream as a decoy.

Enraged by the treachery of it, the frustration,
Glenn screamed, then fired three shots into the storm,
into the swamp, finally made it up the bank out of
the freezing water, crawling up into the snow, his eyes
slits, his no longer placid good dentist's face as
twisted as the trunk of a windblown tree.

Several years earlier, during a tornado or violent
wind storm, two hemlocks had been uprooted, falling
across each other to form a natural chair partially
concealed behind the roots and limbs. It was here
that Norm had collapsed, drained by his run to stay
ahead of Glenn, sitting there watching the first signs
of the storm breaking. Watching Glenn.

And waiting.

No more than fifty feet away Glenn appeared to
circle aimlessly, waving his pistol, shuffling a few steps
in one direction, then in another, several times sticking the gun into his coat pocket and rummaging
through all his pockets, turning them inside out, once
even trying to strike a wet match on the cover. He bellowed, swung his pistol over the terrain and squeezed
off four more shots. He emptied the clip, then re-
loaded . . . "You're around here, Norm. I know
that . . . you hear? I've got time. I'll find you
. . . you *hear?*"

He began running again. His clothes were stiffening. . . . Norm recognized too well the swishing sound made by Glenn's pants legs as they scraped together. His ragged breathing carried even over the wind. With a stiff-legged waddle like a prisoner in leg irons, he disappeared into the brush. . . . A few minutes later he emerged, barely shuffling along, head down, following another furrow of tracks. He staggered past and almost walked into the creek. He halted, shook his head, squinting as he turned in several complete circles. He looked up at the storm, which seemed to be easing, and nodded his head. Then, cutting away from all the tracks, he headed out directly away from the mainland toward the center of the seven-mile swamp. He paused abruptly, then turned and headed back toward Norm. Fifty feet away, with Norm clearly visible if only he would look up, Glenn turned a third time and disappeared into the swamp.

The wind howled through the forest. A few last snowflakes slashed through the waving branches of the hemlocks. The swish, swish sound of Glenn's frozen pants legs faded and died away. Surely, it seemed to Norm, within minutes Glenn would freeze.

CHAPTER XXII

By dusk the storm had broken up. Overhead, low fluffy clouds were scattering, scuttling quickly east as though racing to catch up with the main part of the storm. In the west, pink and red radiated halfway to the zenith, the colors pure in the clear winter air. The picture changed before Norm's eyes with a wondrous display. The world around him, clouds racing, carrying with them coats of pink, poplars standing proud and naked with their tops bathed in red, and low on the horizon a wall of red glimmering, limitless like a rainbow, without beginning or end, only the illusion of it.

Something ticked at the back of Norm's head . . . a hint of noise, an intimation . . . he couldn't be sure. He jerked his cap off to hear better. It echoed in his head, a faint sound like one branch rubbing against another, carrying from the swamp where Glenn had disappeared. But Glenn should be down by now. Norm dismissed the sound as part of his imagination, his fatigue, the lingering effects of the fear after his last bullet had spun off into the forest over Glenn's diving form. He'd made quite a run . . . lunging through deep snow, circling

through that swamp, his lungs on fire as he struggled
to stay ahead of Glenn.

He turned his attention now back to the forest.
High in the east, between openings in the low rushing clouds, the sheen of a three-quarter moon drew
his eye, the promise of a bitter cold night. A deep arc-
tic high was pushing in behind the tremendous low
of the storm. In a half hour it would be completely
clear, the temperature sliding well below zero by
dawn. It would be a beautiful winter night, Norm
knew, his favorite kind, with the moon shedding pale
blue light on the carpet of snow.

To his right, down about a hundred feet and
clearly visible now, was the finger of high land that
Glenn had been unable to see, jutting down into the
swamp, almost meeting the spot where the five-feet-
wide swamp creek meandered toward an unseen pond
a half mile out. The stream was open, the water
black in the dim light like freshly rolled blacktop.
Logs had fallen back and forth across the creek, their
roots gradually eaten away by the slowly moving
water. On the opposite side of the creek, the dead
remnants of old pine trees jutted ten to fifteen feet
into the sky—gray, worn stumps without limbs, rotting
at the roots, dark fingers in the dusk, fading monu-
ments to a forest that once had been. Where Glenn
had disappeared, only the trees and snow were visible.

It was a world of his own. Here, in this tiny swamp
glen, no one expected him to *be* anything, to act any
particular way. Here he was free.

And what would happen when he told his story?
They'd maybe even arrest him, put him in handcuffs
and haul him off to jail. Twelve people dead, two by
his hand in self-defense, the others slaughtered in
cold blood. What a story, nationwide. But once the
evidence was examined, they'd set him free. Wouldn't
they? Maybe not. Manslaughter was a possible charge,

at least for Rod. He could see the faces, cameras, the
click of handcuffs binding his wrists, the cement cell,
the questions, the cursing . . . Barbara and Glenn
Sr., and on and on, with always the sad shaking of
heads . . . and Joannie, and Kim, and Jeffrey,
what would they think—?

Stop it, he ordered himself. Stop giving up, damn
you. . . . He shivered, a gentle shaking that gradually increased until it rattled his teeth and shook his
joints. He leaned back, almost forgetting the swamp
where Glenn had disappeared.

After a time his shivering subsided, only to return
in more violent spasms, racking him from head to
foot. Then the time between shakes gradually length-
ened, the tentacles of cold seeping into his flesh fading and becoming almost warm, bringing a kind of
contentment like the first days of his love with Joannie when she'd so admired him and looked on him as
her big kind savior. Such days. Old homely Norm in
love with a beautiful girl who loved him. . . .

He nodded, surprised to discover he'd almost been
sleeping, drifting away quietly as though without a
care in the world, the warm sun making him doze as
the yellow rays soaked into the skin, the swish, swish,
swish like the slap of waves against the shore or of
branches rubbing against each other or—

Swish, swish, swish. It went off in his mind like an
alarm. He turned, a movement of astonished slow motion. *"Glenn."*

He stood no more than twenty feet away, teetering
back and forth, staring as he pointed the Luger,
clasped in the icebound grip of one bare hand. He
shivered violently. His clothes were stiff, flaked with
crystals of ice at the knee and elbow joints. He'd lost
his hat. The hair thin on the side of his head was stiff
and brittle. He appeared an alien being, his lips
wrinkled and swollen, unmoving like the pink and
blued skin of the rest of his face, the white of the

frostbitten areas scattered across it like large splotches of paint. Only his eyes still glistened with life. He tried to speak, managing only a kind of wailing moan.

Norm strained to escape the numbing sensation that he was dreaming. And as in a dream he thought rather than said what he felt. . . . No, Glenn, not another one . . . my god, enough killing. . . . But of course he got none of this out as he watched, transfixed, Glenn bring the Luger to bear. He drew back, trying to suck himself into a smaller target, as the black bore centered on his chest. Glenn's curled hand was almost white from frostbite. Norm watched as the hand jerked, pulled by the arm. He fell backward off his perch. Again, and once again, the hand jerked. Nothing happened. Not even the click of the hammer. The mechanism had frozen.

Glenn teetered, staring at the pistol, then slumped backward into the snow, his back against a stump, his bare hands resting on his lap, his chin against his chest as he gazed at the pistol frozen in his hand. He rocked gently back and forth, cradling the gun as though it were a baby, grunting rhythmically.

Norm edged back up onto his seat, half turned sideways. He eyed Glenn, who had become silent.

"Glenn . . . ?"

The forest echoed with its quiet.

Norm looked more closely. Glenn's eyes were open, unseeing. The glistening had faded. The eyes were glazed over, covered now by a dull film such as he had seen too often on the eyes of a dead buck. . . .

So it was over.

His hip burned deep, he could feel the sticky flow of blood from the wrenched-open wound on the back of his arm. He hurt: legs, back, arm, lungs, head. They all hurt.

He thought of Joannie, her smiles, her poise as she moved about a warm, brightly decorated room at a cocktail party, a very pretty woman who came out just right—not overdressed, not overanxious. Just right, a kind of science Norm knew he could never master. And he thought of Kim, the daughter who steered around him as an experienced canoeist would avoid a solitary boulder in a wide stream; and of his son Jeffrey, the hermit with his science fiction and a generational disinterest in anything else, including his own future.

He tried not to think of Norm Petrie, of the man he'd shot, of the corpse in front of him.

After several moments he looked up. The last lingering traces of the sun had faded, leaving only the pale three-quarter moon. In the clear, cold air the moon stood out, giving the illusion of daylight. Except there were shadows in the snow and blackness in the walls of brush where he could not see clearly, and there was the thick carpet of snow, pale blue now in the moonlight, with thousands of tiny ice crystals sparkling like gems. Farther out in the swamp the gray stumps of the dead pines jutted defiantly into the purple sky, rising out of the clouds of thick mist that filtered off the cold, brackish water of the tiny swamp creek where it met the even colder air—

Which now rustled. Norm slowly turned his head sideways to see a white snow owl cupping its huge wings and gliding onto a perch in the upper limbs of a nearby tree. He also caught the fleeting shadow of a snowshoe rabbit crossing an opening in the tag alders to his left.

He sat quietly beneath the snow owl. The two of them watched over the tiny moonlit opening. Twice more he saw the rabbit moving quickly, staying near brush as if aware of the snow owl in the tree. Once, on the far side of the creek, a doe and a fawn came out of the brush to water, poised in the eerie light of the moon, statues that suddenly turned and moved up the jutting high land finger, floundering in the deep snow, pausing to nibble at tree buds and bark from small saplings.

Something moved nearby, and he turned just in time to see the blur of the owl plunging to the ground. Snow flew, a squealing, and abruptly, with a heavy thrashing of wings, the snow owl lifted into the sky with a snowshoe rabbit dangling from its talons.

Norm leaned back so that his head rested against the upturned trunk of the top hemlock. Then slowly, with effort, he turned his head back toward the glen, to the marks of the scuffle where the rabbit had ventured into the open. The owl had a purpose—kill for survival, which it had finally come down to for him.

He almost slept, following Glenn. But some deeper drive spurred him to stay awake, to respect what he knew. If he slept, Norman Petrie would be no more than the big black, a frozen and forgotten carcass. The only glory was in life. . . .

He fought the fatigue, shaking his head against the cobwebs, squinting to see. One thing he did see . . . the world, at least for him, had changed. He'd had his last hunt—the ultimate, for survival. And with the end of lies, the one of his married life would also have to end. Or rather the pretense of it. It had ended, he now knew, years ago.

And with ballistics technology, plus his wound and the strong claim of self-defense, he just might get his story across. He'd move north to the wilderness he loved. Maybe even up to Canada. Not as a hermit—he needed people too—except sometimes they suffocated him. Too much of them would kill him. Not that he was so special . . . after all, what *really* had killed Glenn? . . .

He thought of the others' faces as he told his tale. Would they understand?

Gingerly he stepped forward into the moonlight, a man returned from the frozen dead. He winced. The pain . . . it felt good.

DOWN RIVER

PETER COLLIER

An American family lives in a brutal world where survival is all.

"Explodes in a life-reaffirming mission so powerful it leaves the reader's heart in his throat."—*San Francisco Herald Examiner.*

"Brilliantly conceived, beautifully written. Nothing less than superb."—*New York Times.*

"A skillful blend of William Faulkner and James Dickey, author of *Deliverance*. Gripping, moving. A very contemporary tale."—*The Houston Post.*

"A book primarily about family, about continuity, about belonging. A true lyrical touch."—*Newsweek.*

A Dell Book $2.75 (11830-1)

BY REASON OF INSANITY

Shane Stevens
author of *Rat Pack* and *Go Down Dead*

"Sensational."—*New York Post*

Thomas Bishop—born of a mindless rape—escapes from an institution for the criminally insane to deluge a nation in blood and horror. Not even Bishop himself knows where—and in what chilling horror—it will end.

"This is Shane Stevens' masterpiece. The most suspenseful novel in years."—Curt Gentry, co-author of *Helter Skelter*

"A masterful suspense thriller steeped in blood, guts and sex."—*The Cincinnati Enquirer*

A Dell Book $2.75   (11028-9)

At your local bookstore or use this handy coupon for ordering:

Comes the Blind Fury

John Saul
Bestselling author of
Cry for the Strangers
and *Suffer the Children*

More than a century ago, a gentle, blind child walked the paths of Paradise Point. Then other children came, teasing and taunting her until she lost her footing on the cliff and plunged into the drowning sea.

Now, 12-year-old Michelle and her family have come to live in that same house—to escape the city pressures, to have a better life.

But the sins of the past do not die. They reach out to embrace the living. Dreams will become nightmares.

Serenity will become terror There will be no escape.

A Dell Book $2.75   (11428-4)

At your local bookstore or use this handy coupon for ordering:

 DELL BOOKS   COMES THE BLIND FURY $2.75   (11428-4)
P.O. BOX 1000, PINEBROOK, N.J. 07058

Please send me the above title. I am enclosing $ _____
(please add 75¢ per copy to cover postage and handling). Send check or money order—no cash or C.O.D.'s. Please allow up to 8 weeks for shipment.

Mr/Mrs/Miss _____

Address _____

City _____ State/Zip _____